Praise for *Flight of No Return*

"Mike Paull's final novel in the Brett Raven trilogy is one of his best and proves he truly understands the secret to writing a good mystery. He leads the reader along, gradually filling in the missing pieces without giving too much away, and then springs a surprise ending. This book is a real page turner and impossible to put down."

Lloyd Rogers,
Author... Having Carlota

...

"With Flight of No Return *author Mike Paull has treated the reader to an exciting completion to the Brett Raven Trilogy series. It is full of suspense, interesting new characters, and life and death situations. Because Brett is both a dentist and a pilot, Mike has cleverly woven those activities into his very circuitous plot. This well written story, full of intrigue and dangerous predicaments, is a 'must read' for lovers of a good mystery."*

Douglas L. Bockus,
Author...WWII true story, Fortress Down

ALSO BY MIKE PAULL

Flight of Betrayal
Brett Raven Mystery book I

Flight of Deception
Brett Raven Mystery book II

Tales from the Sky Kitchen Cafe
Aviation based short stories

Flight of No Return

Mike Paull

Published by Skyhawk Publishing
Printed in the USA
Design by Carla Resnick
ISBN 9780985874353
Library of Congress Catalog Number 2014912371

FLIGHT OF NO RETURN

To my father, Hank, whose life was cut too short at age forty-seven, and to my mother, Irene, who loved him every day for the rest of her life.

"You have to learn the rules of the game. And then you have to play better than anyone else."

–Albert Einstein

FLIGHT OF NO RETURN

Prologue

New York City, N.Y.
August 30, 2001

Patrick O'Hara was in his twentieth year with the New York City Police Department and his eighth as a homicide detective in the Midtown South Precinct. The late shift was almost over, when his partner Al Czychowitz put a cup of coffee on his desk. "Pat, wake up. 'Looks like we do overtime tonight, there's been a shooting at the Times Square Hotel."

The sound of the ceramic mug echoing off the plastic desktop roused Pat from his catnap. "Damn, two weeks without smoking and all I want to do is sleep. What time is it anyway?

"Five minutes to twelve."

"Can't the next shift take it?"

"Not here yet. Lieutenant said to me, 'this one's yours.'"

Pat pulled his rumpled corduroy jacket off the corner of his chair and managed to down a large gulp from the steaming mug. "Ouch, that's hot," he said, fanning his mouth with his hand.

"You okay?' Al asked.

"Yeah, fine," he replied, still trying to cool his tongue. "Let's take the Ford."

O'Hara pulled into the red zone on 46th St. near Broadway and parked behind an ambulance where three paramedics were leaning on its hood, each holding a Starbucks cup and laughing quietly. "You guys look bored," he said.

A well-built guy dressed in beige scrubs and a dark blue vest with yellow E.M.T. letters on the front looked over at him. "Not much use for us," he replied. "This one's going to the morgue."

The Times Square Hotel was small with only eighty rooms and twelve suites. It certainly wasn't a five star, but it might get at least three from Travel and Leisure, no more than two and a half from Condé Nast. Pat and Al made their way to the narrow elevator near the rear of the small lobby, slid the folding iron gate open, got in, and rode to the fifth floor.

The door to room 561 was open, but it was well protected by a yellow crime scene tape and a uniformed cop. The detectives flashed their gold shields and the uniform waved them through. The body was lying face up on the carpet in front of an overturned table chair, and the medical examiner was bending over it. "What's it look like?" Pat asked.

The pathologist glanced up. "Oh, how you doin', O'Hara? Pretty grim, one shot through the forehead."

Al put on a pair of rubber gloves and bent down over the body. "Looks like a clean shot, think it's a hit?"

"I don't think so, there's a shell casing next to the body. Most professionals collect that shit before they leave, don't they?"

"Usually, I guess," Al shrugged. "Kind of a startled look on the victim's face, like the shot came as a surprise." He bent down for a better look at the body. "Is that a fresh cut above the right eyebrow?"

The M.E. gave a closer look. "Yeah, I didn't notice that, guess I'm getting tired."

Just as O'Hara began to slip on a set of gloves, a photographer and a forensics team arrived and went to work recording the crime scene. A camera lit up the room with sporadic flashes, and fingerprint dust was circulating through the air. A half hour later as the entourage finished packing up their equipment, the photographer turned to Pat and said, "It's all yours, man, good luck."

O'Hara gave him a half smile and bent down to pick up the shell casing, which he dropped into a plastic bag he pulled from his pocket. "Looks like about 9 mil," he said to Al. "Definitely a pistol."

Czychowitz nodded in agreement. "We know anything about the victim?" he asked the doctor, who by now was looking exhausted and ready for bed.

"That's your department, you're the detective, go and detect."

"Thanks doc," he said, as he joined Pat to walk the suite.

"Looks like the place has been wiped pretty clean," O'Hara said, as he used a rubber coated finger to open the desk drawer. "Why don't you take the little bedroom, I'll do the big one,"

Czychowitz acknowledged with a head nod and disappeared through the door leading to the smaller bedroom. He couldn't believe how clean the bedroom and bath were, almost like the maid had just been there. As his eyes scoured the white tile floor, something caught his eye. It was lying in the corner just behind the wastebasket and its brown color stood out against the light floor. He picked it up and recognized a prescription bottle with most of the label scratched off.

Al joined Pat in the other bedroom. "Notice anything strange?" Pat asked, as he spotted him in the doorway.

"Yeah, clean as whistle but no towels around. Whoever cleaned up must have used them and taken them away when they left, probably worried about hair or DNA. This thing looks pretty well planned."

"Agree," Pat said. "Find anything in the other room?"

Take a look at this," Al said, as he handed him the prescription bottle.

O'Hara turned it over in his hand trying to decipher the label. "Surprised they overlooked it, being so thorough and all." He rubbed his finger along the surface trying to smooth the remaining pieces of the wrinkled sticky paper."

"I think it was meant for the trash can, but missed," Al said.

"Wonder what this means? I can barely make out the letters *EENS* on top and *2-85ca* near the bottom," Pat said.

Al glanced at it again but didn't seem too interested. He wasn't really into the cerebral part of being a detective. What he liked most, was pushing guys around a little and being called Sir. "We'll figure it out tomorrow, it's getting late," he said, covering a yawn with his open hand.

O'Hara looked at his watch and dropped the bottle into another plastic baggie. "I'll keep combing the suite. You see what the desk clerk has on this room."

Al approached the front desk and was met by a long haired, sleepy eyed man in his late twenties, who had apparently stayed up during his time off and was now trying desperately to stay awake while back on his shift. Al flashed his badge to wake him from his stupor and said, "Hey man, pull the check-in records for *561*, I need to see 'em."

The clerk summoned enough energy to shoot him a dirty look and went ahead slowly scrolling a computer page and tapping a key which dropped the printer into gear. It pumped out three sheets of data; one with check-in information and two with daily charges. Al studied the top sheet:

Mr. & Mrs. Alfred Hansen
217 Outrigger Ave.
Lakeland, Florida 33810

Check in: August 27, 2001, 3:00 p.m.
Check out: August 31, 2001, 11:00 a.m.
4 night stay
2 Br, 2 Bath Suite w/ Hide a Bed Sofa
$279. per night
$1116. plus 18% state & city tax. $200.88.
$1316.88 Paid in advance-CASH

"Let me see the ledger of charges?" Al said.

The clerk lazily handed him two pages of

accounting. Czychowitz studied them and asked, "What's this charge for $127 earlier this evening?"

"Uh, that's room service," he replied, still trying not to nod off.

"Is there a ticket order that goes with it?" Al inquired.

Sleepy thumbed through a pile of receipts. "Yeah, here it is."

Czychowitz inspected it. There were charges for one chicken and two steak dinners, three salads, two deserts, two beers, and a Diet Coke. "Why didn't anyone sign for it?"

The clerk tapped a couple keys on his board and looked at his screen. "They paid cash, looks like they did that for all their meals."

Al had the clerk make a copy for him and he went back to the fifth floor. "Anything?" O'Hara asked.

"I'm guessing the registration name is a phony, but I'll check it out. 'Looks like three people were living in the suite and eating most of their meals here. Three full dinners were ordered earlier this evening. We just have to figure out who ate them, and who didn't get to finish dessert. You find anything else?"

"Not a hell of a lot, but there were a few scraps of paper under a bed, floating in a pile of dust and mouse turds. One piece had the name *Stovepipe Wells*

LO9 written on it. Any idea what that means?"

Czychowitz scratched his head while stifling another yawn. "Beats me, sounds like a rock band."

THE KIDNAP

2/15/01 – 8/31/01

Chapter One

San Carlos, Ca.
August 27, 2001

Brett was back in his dental office treating patients; it felt good. Six months was a long time to spend with a broken hand and limited to just managing his office without being able to interact with patients. The attack by Mexican gangsters was fading from his memory and replaced with the pleasant thoughts of his re-marriage to Annie and the upcoming birth of twins in October.

Janet, his assistant, was seated next to him at the dental chair busily navigating a suction tube through the patient's mouth, evacuating water from Brett's working area. She glanced away from the patient and spotted Ginger, the office manager, in the doorway trying to get Brett's attention. Janet turned off the suction and removed the tube from the patient's mouth. Brett looked up at her to find the reason for stopping the procedure; she nodded her head toward the treatment room door. Ginger had her index finger curled in the air and was motioning Brett toward the hallway.

Brett apologized to the patient and quickly exited the room. "Ginger, what is it? I'm right in the middle of a procedure."

"Something's up, you better take this phone call," she said, with a frown on her face.

"Can't it wait?" Brett asked.

"Take the call," Ginger said again.

Brett was irritated as he stripped off his gloves and entered his private office. It wasn't like Ginger to interrupt him without good reason, but he couldn't imagine why she had insisted on his taking this call in the middle of a busy morning. The red light on the phone panel was blinking ominously. Brett reached for the receiver and with a feeling of foreboding he punched the button below the light. "Dr. Raven."

The voice on the other end sounded as if it was being delivered through a long tunnel and the cadence was drawn out making each word sound slurred. It was apparent to Brett the distorted voice was coming through a machine the caller was using to disguise the sound. "Go home immediately. Your wife will not be there. Wait for another call," the mutated voice droned, and then the line was dead.

Brett apologized to his patient for a family emergency and sped his Lexus up the hill and hit the 'open' button on the garage remote as soon as he made the turn into the driveway. Annie's car was still in the spot it had occupied when he had left for the office two hours earlier. He opened the door to the living area and wasn't greeted by the familiar beeping of the alarm. "Annie?" he yelled. There was no response. "Annie, are you here?" he hollered again. Again, there was only silence.

Brett raced up the stairs to their bedroom. The bed was unmade, several of Annie's dresser drawers were open, and the light was on in the bathroom. He uttered another inquiry in its direction. "Annie, you in there?" He looked into the room. It was empty.

He scrambled down the stairs to the first level and tried to decipher what was going on. Except for the ticking of the old school clock hanging on the kitchen wall, the house was silent, as he went from room to room in search of some clue where Annie might have gone without taking her car. He found nothing until he noticed the sunlight from a window reflecting off something which had been left on the front hall table. He picked it up; it was the necklace he had given Annie on her thirtieth birthday. She rarely went anywhere without it.

Brett turned the necklace over in his hands and

noticed the little gold heart was missing from the chain. Suddenly he was startled by the shrill ring of the phone. It rang again and then a third time. He picked it up without speaking, just listening to the eerie voice of the machine coming through the earpiece. "Don't bother searching the house," the voice again droned. "Your wife is with us."

"Who is this?" Brett demanded.

"You'll find out soon enough. Go to your aviation charts and locate airport LO9. Fly your plane there tomorrow and make your way into town. Someone will meet you at the Bad Water Saloon at 11 a.m. and oh yes, please don't be stupid enough to call the police, Annie won't be there. By the way, we know where Samantha lives and I'm guessing you don't want her to get a visit from us."

"Tell me who you are," Brett screamed into the phone. All he received back was a dial tone.

Brett felt a wave of nausea as he went to the bookcase over his desk and foraged through his aviation library until he located his *Airport / Facility Directory 2001*, a large light green paperback book, which contained information on every large and small airport in the United States. He removed it from the shelf and thumbed through it until he came to LO9.

L09-Stovepipe Wells, Death Valley California
36°36'22"N 117°08'47"W / 36.60611°N 117.14639°W /
36.60611; -117.14639
Altitude: 25 ft. MSL
Runway 5/23: 3260 ft x 65 ft
Common **Traffic Advisory Frequency**: 122.9
Airport remarks-: Unattended, no fuel available

He tore the page from the book and studied it as he dialed the number for his office.

"Dr. Raven and Gruber's office, Ginger speaking," the familiar voice said.

"Ginger, it's me. I need you to cancel all my appointments for the rest of today and all day tomorrow. Dr. Gruber can take my emergencies"

"Brett, you've only been back a couple months and the schedule is packed, what's up?"

"Annie has disappeared and I'm worried sick. I have to fly down to a little airport in the desert tomorrow."

"Is this what that phone call was about?" Ginger asked.

"Exactly. It directed me to a place called Stovepipe Wells."

"Brett, I thought you were done risking your life after you recovered that money from J.T. and returned it to the insurance companies."

"I thought so too, but it appears the nightmare isn't over. I have to get Annie back safe and sound, and I think this is the way to do it."

"You know J.T.'s involved in this, why are you afraid to just call the police?" Ginger asked.

"That would take a lot of explaining: J.T.'s fraud in Mexico, what I found out about it and some of the questionable things I did in Florida to retrieve the stolen insurance money from him. Besides, they know about Samantha and the babies, and I don't think the police could protect her. Please, Ginger, I need your help"

"Brett, of course I'll help. I'll get the appointments cancelled, but if I don't hear from you by tomorrow night, I'm calling the police."

"Fair enough," Brett replied. "I'll call you as soon as I can."

"Brett?"

"Yes Ginger."

"Please be careful."

"I will, don't worry."

CHAPTER TWO

West Palm Beach, Fla.
February 15, 2001

6 months earlier...

J.T. put down the phone. He was sweaty, shaking, and felt as though the wave of nausea he was experiencing would cause him to vomit any second. Brett Raven had just called and dropped a bomb that almost exploded his brain. "How could I have been so stupid?" he asked himself. He stumbled to the bar and poured himself a half glass of Jack Daniels.

"Who was on the phone?" Maria asked, as she sat down on the sofa. She was gorgeous with her blond hair let down to her shoulders and her shapely legs displayed beneath a short sun dress. "Tony, did you hear me?"

J.T. took a slug of the whiskey, "Yeah, I heard you."

"Well?"

"I, I don't know what to tell you," he said, as he refilled his Old Fashion glass.

"Start by telling me who called and then tell me why you're downing liquor at two in the afternoon."

J.T. felt light headed and eased into an arm chair across from the couch. "It was Brett Raven," he answered.

"Who?"

"You remember, the guy who caught up with us after the insurance scam."

Now Maria began to perspire. "The guy who came to the apartment in Denver? The guy we ran away from in the middle of the night?"

"Yeah, that guy." J.T. answered, while draining his glass.

"Is he after us again?"

"He's been after us for six months, but I just realized he found us a couple months ago."

"I don't get it, why didn't he approach us then?"

J.T. jumped up and ran to the powder room and threw his head in the toilet bowl before he sprayed the floor. He came back into the living room wiping his face with a damp towel. "He did approach us, but we just didn't know it."

"I don't get it."

"You know those people we met, the big drug dealer Carlos, the loan broker Manny, and their wives Marcella and Carmen? They were phonies.

The whole scenario was set up by Brett Raven."

"What do you mean phonies? We had dinner at their estate, traveled with them in their private jet to the Bahamas, became friends."

"It was a con to gain our trust."

"I still don't get it. For what reason?"

"Raven wanted to get hold of those insurance funds we received."

Maria's brain went into alarm mode. "Tony, you've never told me the whole story about the insurance scam, have you?"

J.T. was feeling nauseous again and made another trip to the toilet. When he returned Maria was crying. "No," he said. "I tried to make it easier for you."

"I think it's time you tell me. Now!" she said, defiantly.

J.T. wiped the perspiration from his upper lip with his right wrist. "Two guys supposedly died in that plane crash in Baja: Tony Russo and J.T. Talbot."

"I know who Tony Russo is, you, my husband. Who was J.T. Talbot?"

"That was my name before I married you. I was best friends with Brett Raven until I married his ex-wife Annie after they divorced."

Maria's eyes were as wide as saucers. "Married? When did you divorce her?" she asked.

J.T. was silent.

I asked, "When did you divorce her?"

"I never did. I figured since both 'me's' were going to perish in that crash it was unnecessary."

"So you were married to both of us at the same time?"

"I didn't think it would be a problem. I left a $5 million life insurance to her as well as the $5.5 million you got. I figured it would be a win, win for everyone."

"Then why is her ex-husband chasing us?"

"He figured out what caused the plane crash and how I faked the deaths. He told Annie and she apparently wanted to give the money back to the insurance companies. Brett hates my guts and wanted to get control of our insurance money and return it to the companies."

The reality was beginning to sink in with Maria. "Are you telling me he was successful?"

"Those con men, Carlos and Manny, talked me into investing $5.25 million into a short term investment that would double our money within ninety days."

"All our money is gone?" Maria shrieked.

J.T. looked straight down at the floor. "Most of it," he said softly.

Maria got off the couch and went to the chair where J.T. was sitting. She slapped her right hand across his left cheek with all the force she had in her arm. "You son of a bitch! You were married to me and that other woman at the same time, you talked me into being an accomplice to a fraud, and then loaned away our money without even asking me."

J.T. rubbed his cheek; he could feel a welt forming. "I can't believe I fell for it. I'm so sorry."

"Sorry won't cut it. How much do we have left?"

"I guess he felt a little compassionate. He left us about $300 thousand in the account."

"Get the Merrill Lynch check book," she demanded.

J.T went into the den and returned with a vinyl covered folder. "What do you want it for?"

"Write me a check for $150 thousand. I'm going to pack my things."

"Maria, you can't. Where will you go? Where will I go?"

"You can go straight to hell as far as I'm concerned."

"He said a tough insurance detective named Biff Erskine is being sent after us."

"Yeah, well say hello to him for me," Maria said, as she walked out of the room and pulled two suitcases from the front hall closet.

Chapter Three

San Carlos, Ca.
August 28, 2001

Brett tossed and turned all night and rolled out of bed with less than two hours sleep, a few minutes before the alarm was set to wake him. He spread his aviation charts over the dining room table and plotted a course to Stovepipe Wells. Airport LO9 was located in the northeast sector of Death Valley near the California-Nevada border and the straight line distance from San Carlos was 287 miles.

He previously had owned a large twin engine Beech Baron 58; however, his partner J.T, Talbot had crashed it in Baja Mexico over a year ago. The Baron D55 which Brett was now flying was bought for him by Annie. It was smaller than the 58, but faster. With its dual 285 hp engines and a speed of 225 mph, he calculated it would take him less than an hour and a half to fly from San Carlos to

Stovepipe Wells.

The directions Brett received from the phone call instructed him to be at the saloon by 11 a.m. He performed a pre-flight of his plane at 8 o'clock and was in the air by 8:30. The 1969 Baron had been re-fitted with all the up to date instruments and avionics except for a GPS unit. He had immediately invested in a slick portable unit, a Garmin 295, which he now programmed for a direct route to Death Valley.

His heading was almost due east. He set the autopilot for an eight, six, zero, degree heading and a rate of climb of a thousand feet per minute, he then dialed in frequency 124.4. "Norcal approach, Baron Six, Seven, Five, Nine, Mike, request."

His headset received an immediate response. "Baron Six, Seven, Five, Nine, Mike, go ahead with your request."

"Five, Nine, Mike, off San Carlos eastbound. Request flight following to Stovepipe Wells at ninety-five hundred feet."

There was a silence and then the controller said, "Stovepipe what?"

Brett smiled, "Sorry, it's Stovepipe Wells and the identifier is Lima, Zero, Niner."

"Okay, I've got it. I've been a controller for eighteen years and this is the first time I've even heard of that airport."

"Join the club," Brett responded.

Now the controller laughed. "Squawk 5353 on your transponder and clear to climb to nine thousand five hundred through class Bravo airspace.

"Cleared through class Bravo to ninety-five, Brett repeated."

"By the way," the controller added. "You'll have several military operation areas on your route."

"I see that," Brett answered. "I'll check to make sure they're not hot."

"Good flight," the controller added and signed off.

In order to reach Death Valley, Brett would have to cross over or near some of the highest peaks of the Sierra Nevada mountain range. He checked his sectional chart which indicated the maximum peak was fourteen thousand eight hundred feet. After passing north of Fresno, he requested an altitude of fifteen thousand five hundred and set his autopilot for a climb rate of five hundred feet per minute, after which he requested a temporary change of radio frequency, and dialed in 126.55. "Joshua approach, Baron Six, Seven, Five, Nine, Mike."

"Five, Nine, Mike, this is Joshua."

"Five, Nine, Mike is at fifteen five for Stovepipe Wells. We're going to penetrate the Foothill, Owens, and Saline MOA's, any action in there this morning?"

"You're okay if you stay at or below sixteen; it's hot at sixteen-five and higher."

"Thanks for the help, Five, Nine, Mike." Brett turned on his oxygen unit and placed a cannula under his nose for his flight time above fourteen thousand feet.

When his GPS indicated sixty miles from Stovepipe, Brett set a descent rate of a thousand feet per minute and started a visual scan for the airport. In ten minutes as the Baron descended through five thousand feet, he spotted what looked like a postage stamp in the heart of Death Valley. He tweaked his heading for a straight in landing on runway zero five.

Stovepipe Wells, Ca.

After parking on a little patch of blacktop designated 'ramp', Brett shut down his engines. The only other plane on the tarmac was a Cessna 172 with a decal on its side panel that read, *Freedom Flight Center, Henderson, Nevada*. He opened the door and was greeted with a blast of hot air. It was only 10 a.m. and already the temperature was at ninety-three degrees; it was forecast to reach one-nineteen. The airport looked as if it was rarely used. Weeds were sprouting through cracks in the runway and taxiway, and the lone small building on the property was locked with a sign on the door that read: *In case of emergency call Death Valley Park Ranger, 760-786-3245.* There was a pay phone attached to the weathered siding of the building, apparently for those without a cell.

The blacktop had a few embedded tie-down ropes that Brett used to secure the Baron against any upcoming wind. He locked it up and began the half mile walk into town. About a block away from the airport he met up with a young clean cut looking guy headed in the opposite direction back toward the airport. "That your 172 tied down at the airport?" Brett asked.

The young man smiled. "Yeah, just flew in from Vegas. Want to get that little Cessna out of here before it gets too hot for its small engine to get me off the ground."

"Good luck," Brett said, and continued walking.

There wasn't much to see in the town of Stovepipe Wells. The main drag looked like a hundred year old scene from a movie set of fake store fronts. The two blocks of Main Street consisted of a motel, gas station, general store, gift shop, ranger station, a restaurant and a saloon. Brett headed straight for the Badwater Saloon.

As he passed by the Standard Station there was a bent over, old man with a gray beard using an outdated manual gas pump to fill his pickup. Next door the Toll Road Restaurant had a sign displayed: *Open at 11:30 – Maybe.* The saloon building looked as if it was barely standing. The wood pillars supporting the front porch roof were bending under the weight of the logs which were put together overhead with the use of old fashion wooden dowels. There were no western style swinging saloon doors; probably with the invention of air conditioning they had been replaced with the single solid wood door that creaked and groaned as Brett pushed it inward. He entered the old wooden structure half expecting to see a bunch of tough cowboys slumped over the bar, but he was mistaken. The interior décor, however, was definitely old west. Deer antlers decorated the walls along with old black and white faded photographs of unsmiling men in huge cowboy hats. Two buckboard wagon wheels hung from the ceiling, each holding a dozen bare bulbs, which illuminated the windowless room. The only two occupants were a young man in shorts and a tee shirt who was sweeping the beer stained hardwood floor and an old man dressed in jeans and a Standard Oil work shirt, chugging coffee from a chipped porcelain mug.

"Help ya?" The young guy asked.

"How 'bout a coke, I'm supposed to meet someone here at eleven."

Brett took a seat at the old wooden bar and leaned over the tarnished brass rails as the young man popped the top of a Pepsi can and poured it into a glass filled with ice cubes. "Not many tourists this time of year," he said, while sizing Brett up. "Too hot."

"I just flew in. Hope to get out before the temp hits a hundred," Brett said, as he began downing the soft drink.

"Your name Raven, by any chance?"

Brett put down his glass. "How did you know that?" he asked, with his warning antenna on high beam.

"A pilot was just here and left an envelope; said to give it to a guy named Raven. Guess that be you." The young man reached under the bar and retrieved a manila envelope.

"Thanks," Brett said, as he took his glass and the envelope, retreated to a table away from the bar, and tore it open and emptied its contents onto the stained wood top. A dozen photos fanned out and were followed by a folded single sheet of typewritten paper.

As he began to examine the photos the acid in his stomach rose to the back of his tongue. They were close-up images of Samantha's face and protruding belly. He dropped the pictures onto the table top, his hand noticeably shaking, and unfolded the paper and peered down at it.

Equity in townhouse-------------$900,000
Retirement plan------------------$800,000
Dental equipment---------------$300,000
Have the $2,000,000 in packets of $100 bills.
If you want to protect your babies and want to see
Annie again, suck it up and start liquidating. You have
7 days to get the money together. Don't fuck with us.
We mean it!

Brett stuffed the paper and the photos into his pocket, left three dollars on the table and broke into a trot back to the airport.

By the time he settled back into the Baron, sweat was pouring off his face and his shirt was stained with rings of perspiration. The engines were still hot, making them difficult to start, but once he got both props spinning, it was a quick taxi back to runway five where he took off, and headed east toward Henderson, a suburb of Las Vegas.

Brett set the letters KHND, the identifier for Henderson Executive airport, into the little 295 GPS unit. The screen indicated 102 miles to the airport and the time en route, twenty-eight minutes. He looked at his watch; he would be there by twelve-thirty.

Henderson, Nevada

Henderson Executive is a busy airport where most of the general aviation pistons and jets land, if they want to avoid Las Vegas McCarran

International. As Brett exited the runway onto the taxiway he called ground control on 127.8. "Five, Nine, Mike off the active, I'm unfamiliar. Can you direct my taxi to the Freedom Flight Center?"

"No problem," the ground controller said. "Right on Charlie, right on Alpha and left on Delta."

"Rodger that, thanks, Five, Nine, Mike."

Brett shut the engines down and made his way to the lobby of the Flight Center. "Help ya?" a cute blonde in a tank top and cut-off shorts asked.

"Yeah, could you have both tanks topped off with a hundred low lead?"

"Sure 'nough, anything else I can help ya with?"

"As a matter of fact there is. Do you know who flew that Cessna 172 over to Death Valley this morning?" he asked, pointing to the little high wing airplane parked in front of the hangar.

The young girl's smile disappeared. "Why, is somethin' wrong?"

Brett put a twenty dollar bill on the counter. "No, sorry to scare you, I just have to know who paid for the charter to deliver an envelope to me at Stovepipe Wells."

The blonde looked relieved. "I thought for a minute Josh dinged the plane or somethin'. I actually booked that charter. A guy came in with the envelope, paid me $300 hundred cash for the charter, gave me instructions to leave it at the saloon for a guy named Raven and then he walked out."

"Did you give him a receipt?" Brett asked.

"Sure," she said, as she thumbed through a short stack of notes. "Here it is, John Andersen," she said, pulling it from the pile and handing it over to Brett.

Brett reached into his wallet and pulled out an old photo of himself with Annie and J.T. He placed it in front of the girl and pointed to J.T. "Is that the guy, John Andersen?"

The blonde laughed. "Not even close, that guy in the picture is good looking. John Andersen was fat with short hair, and had a big scar on his cheek."

Brett took another twenty out of his pocket and handed it to the girl. "Thanks a million," he said. "Buy your boyfriend dinner tonight."

While he was waiting for the Baron to be re-fueled he dialed his office number on his cell. "Dr. Raven and Dr. Gruber's office, Ginger speaking."

"Hi Ginger, I'm headed home without any bullet holes. 'See you tomorrow morning."

"Thank God! Can you tell me about it?"

"We'll talk tomorrow. 'See you at 8 a.m."

CHAPTER FOUR

San Francisco, Ca.
February 16, 2001

6 months earlier...

Elmer Erskine, who answered to the name Biff, hated Brett Raven. Brett had almost gotten him killed by the gangsters who were helping Raven beat him to the recovery of $5.5 million, funds which J.T. Talbot had swindled from insurance companies. If Biff had recovered that money, he would have had the biggest payday of his life, almost $350 thousand. Now Raven was throwing him a bone. He gave Biff, Talbot's address, and if he could find him and bring him back, Biff would still get $100 thousand as the bounty. It certainly wasn't chump change, but still was a lot less than he had expected from this case.

Biff was a private investigator specializing in recovering money from swindlers who had duped insurance companies. He had eked out a meager living while waiting for the golden goose to appear. It finally did, but thanks to Raven it had flown away without him.

Ten years ago Biff carried two hundred and forty pounds of muscle on his six foot five frame. He had a full head of hair and was the target of every woman he met. The person looking back at him from the mirror was not that guy. Biff had put on a hundred and thirty-five pounds and it all had deposited as fat. He had lost most of his hair and now sported a buzz cut to hide it. In addition, he had a jagged scar across his left cheek, compliments of Desert Storm.

"Fuck," he yelled at the reflection, while picking up a bottle of Old Spice and hurling it at the mirror. Blood spots appeared on his legs as chards of glass exploded onto the floor. "Fuck, fuck this," he said, as he walked out of the bathroom and pulled an overnight case out of his closet. It went through his mind that Raven was screwing him over, having him chase his tail in circles, but he had no choice, he had to go.

The red-eye out of San Francisco got him into Miami at eight-forty in the morning Florida time. He hadn't had a paycheck in over a year and he really didn't want to spend the money for a big rental car, but just in case he got lucky and had to drive his catch back to California, he opted for a Chevy Tahoe. "Seventy-five bucks a day, shit!" he mumbled under his breath.

West Palm Beach, Fla.

It took a little over an hour to drive to West Palm Beach. As he reached the outskirts, he rummaged through his pants pocket for the note he had scribbled when Raven had called him. J.T. was going by the name of Antonio Russ and the address where he and his wife Maria were living was 27 Everglade Court. He circled the address on the map that had been given to him at the Hertz counter.

Biff pulled the Tahoe to the curb in the upscale neighborhood, about thirty yards down the street from number twenty-seven. He reached into his case and pulled out a loose fitting sweat shirt and his 9 mm Beretta which he tucked into a holster on the back of his belt; he put on the shirt and draped it over the holster.

He climbed the five stairs to the front porch of the condo, took a wad of gum from his mouth and squeezed it into the peep hole, and gave a solid knock on the door. "Come on in," a man's voice bellowed.

Biff removed the Beretta from the holster, flipped the safety off, and opened the door.

"I'm in the living room," the voice yelled. Biff put his left hand next to his right so that both were steadying the gun as he entered the well-furnished room.

Sitting on the leather couch was a handsome man in his fifties, sipping whisky from an old fashion glass. "The bar's over there," he said, pointing to a countertop next to a walnut bookcase. "Pour yourself a drink. I've been expecting you."

Biff was perplexed. "You J.T. Talbot or Antonio Russ or whatever the fuck you're calling yourself now?"

"Biff you can put down the gun, I'm a swindler not a killer."

"You knew I was coming?" Biff asked.

"Oh yeah, Raven told me."

"Why would he do that?"

"We used to be friends. I guess he felt sorry for me and wanted to give me a chance to get a head start on you."

"Why didn't you?"

J.T. got up and went to the bar. "What will you have, Scotch or Bourbon?"

Biff put the Beretta back in the holster. "Got any Jack?"

"Sure do, sit down, we're going to talk."

Biff chose an armchair facing the couch. J.T. handed him a glass filled halfway up with golden brown liquid. "Where's your wife?" Biff asked.

"I'm afraid she didn't want to wait around to meet you. She left last night."

"For good?"

"Who knows, time will tell," J.T. answered.

Biff took a slug of the whisky. "Why didn't you run with her?"

"I've got a much better idea."

"Yeah, and what might that be?" Biff asked sarcastically.

"How much do you get to bring me back?"

"None of your fuckin' business."

"Come on Biff, what's the difference to you if I know?"

Biff took a slug of his sour mash and sat silently thinking. "A hundred K," he finally said.

"What if I offered you a hundred and fifty and you just head home?"

"Forget it; I'm not breaking the law for an extra fifty, which after taxes comes closer to thirty."

"What is the number then? Two hundred? Two fifty? How 'bout a million tax free?"

"Where the fuck you going to get that kind of dough? I heard Raven cleaned you out."

"Answer my question first. How about one million dollars?"

Maybe the golden goose had shown up after all. "Sure, I'll take a million."

"You willing to do a little work for it?" J.T. asked, while finishing the last drop of scotch from his glass.

"I'm not afraid of work." Biff said.

"How about dirty work? Are you afraid of that?"

"For a million dollars, I'd assume some of the work would be dirty."

"We're going to get two million dollars from your old buddy Brett Raven. Are you okay with that?"

Biff choked on his bourbon. "That bastard is no friend of mine. I'd like nothing more than to relieve him of a couple million dollars."

"It will take me about six months to get everything in place. Will you trust me that long?"

Biff looked skeptical. "How do I know you just won't skip on me?"

"If I wanted to run, I'd have done it yesterday. I need a partner and you're the perfect guy. We both need the money and we both hate Raven. All I need is some time and some space from you to get this going."

Biff went over to the bar and poured another generous helping of Jack Daniels into his glass. He stood at the bar sizing up J.T. and then said, "I'll kill you if you cross me."

J.T. followed Biff to the bar and poured himself

another two fingers of Scotch. "To a profitable partnership," he said, as he tapped Biff's glass.

J.T. spent an hour explaining the plan they would use to extract the money from Brett and his wife Annie. "Thanks for the drinks," Biff said, as he shook J.T.'s hand and started back toward the Tahoe. He was so pleased with himself, he didn't even notice the person watching the house from a car across the street.

CHAPTER FIVE

New York City, N.Y.
August 31, 2001

It was the first hour of their shift and Pat and Al each grabbed a cup of coffee from the precinct snack room. "Forensics in yet on the Time Square shooting?" Al asked.

"Yeah, they just dropped them on my desk."

Both detectives strolled lazily back to their desks, which were located next to each other, and O'Hara picked up two manila folders. He kept one for himself and tossed the other in front of Czychowitz. "It was a Beretta," Pat said. "Did records search that name and address in Florida?"

"Just like I thought, it's a phony," Al replied.

They both continued studying the reports in the folders. "Three sets of prints," Pat said. "One from a guy named John Thomas Talbot, one from a guy named Elmer Erskine, and one from a person unknown."

"Any of the prints match the victim?"

"Oh yeah."

"What do you make of the pill bottle and the note we found?" Al asked.

O'Hara opened his drawer and emptied the contents of his plastic collection bags on his desk. "I can't figure either one out. Let's get that gal with the big jugs up here from forensics. If anyone can figure it out, she can."

Brenda didn't look like the stereotypical forensic nerd. She had a gorgeous face and a figure to match. As she strolled through the door, there were twelve eyes belonging to the six other detectives in the room, following her every step as she approached Pat and Al. "At ease, guys," Pat announced.

Brenda looked unfazed as she hiked her skirt over her knees and sat down at Pat's desk. "What's up?" she asked.

"We're stuck on a couple pieces of evidence. Give us a hand?"

"If I can, sure."

Pat handed Brenda the pill bottle. "The only thing left of the label is EENS and three numbers and two letters, *2-85ca*. We need to know who this prescription belonged to."

She turned it over in her hand and smiled, "Buy me a beer if I give you the answer?"

"Buy you two if you do it quick."

Brenda laughed, "What pharmacy name ends in EENS?"

Both cops sat scratching their heads. "I don't get it." Al said.

"How about Walgreens?" Brenda said, still grinning.

Al grabbed the bottle and looked at it. "Shit, that was too easy, how'd we miss it?"

"Okay," Pat said. "That's one beer, but what are those numbers?"

"I'm not positive, but I'm guessing the ca is a geographic code of some sort and the 2-85 are the last three digits of the prescription number. I'd get hold of their corporate offices and see if you can match the numbers to someone."

"Brenda, I'd give you a big kiss, but every guy in the room would be jealous. We owe you a couple beers, thanks." O'Hara said.

"No problem," she replied, and then kissed him on the cheek and headed for the door.

"Hey, Brenda," Pat called out before she reached the door, "Take a look at one more thing." He took out the paper which had, *Stovepipe Wells L09*, scribbled on it. "Any idea what this might refer to?"

Brenda studied the scribble. "You'll have to figure that one out for yourself, I have no idea," she said, and slipped out through the door.

Pat turned to Al. "I'll call Walgreens, you follow up on the prints."

Deerfield, Illinois was an hour behind New York, giving O'Hara plenty of time to track down the prescription. A pleasant receptionist answered his call. "Walgreens Corporate, how may I help you?"

"My name is detective Pat O'Hara, with the New York City Police Department, Homicide Division. I need to talk with the person in charge of prescription records."

"Please hold, detective," the receptionist said, as elevator music filled the earpiece.

The music stopped. "This is Michael Coleman, what can I do for you, detective?"

"I need to track one of your prescriptions." Pat replied.

"Detective O'Hara, I'll need you to fax me your credentials before I can release any of that information to you."

"I need it right away. Can you stay on the line while I send the fax?"

"No problem, 224-555-2700, I'm right in front of the machine."

Pat took out their standard form and quickly filled it in. He fed it into the fax along with his personal credentials. "Comin' through?" he said, into the phone.

"Got it and it looks good. What do you need?" Coleman asked.

"I have a partial number off one of your script bottles. I was hoping you could narrow the patient down to a list of names."

"My computer is open, give me the numbers."

Pat read the label out loud. "2-85ca."

"Okay, the ca means it was filled in California, and the last two digits, 85, identify the exact pharmacy. It was filled at the San Carlos, California store. There are three digits missing from the front end of the number 2."

"How many prescriptions are possible hits with what you have?"

"Looks like twenty-eight."

"Could you fax me the names, addresses and phone numbers?" Pat asked.

"No problem, give me your number."

Al went to the computer and opened the country-wide data base that matches finger prints to individual stats.

John Thomas Talbot
Financial Consultant
Last known address - 2715 El Mira, Atherton, Ca.
DOB 6/13/1948
Deceased 3/2/2000

Mike Paull

Elmer Erskine
Private Investigator - Insurance
Last known address - 3206 California St. #5, San
Francisco, Ca.
DOB 2/16/1965

"What did you come up with?" Pat asked Al.

"Both from Northern California and one supposedly died last year. How 'bout you?"

O'Hara threw a fax on Al's desk. "The pills were from a pharmacy also in Northern California. Our mystery person is one of these twenty-eight names. Wonder how those three in the hotel room were connected."

"We'll find out. Let's start through your list and put a name on that last set of prints." Al said.

O'Hara and Czychowitz split the list and went to the phones. "This is the New York Police Department. Has anyone in your household been missing or been on a trip to New York City in the last three days?"

Ten of the first twelve calls were answered and didn't yield any results. The thirteenth call, made by Al raised suspicion. "I'm sorry, who are you again?" the voice asked?

"I'm detective Czychowitz, New York City Police Department, homicide division. May I have your name sir?"

"My name is Dr. Brett Raven. Wh...why are

you calling me?"

"I can't tell you that doctor, but I need to know if anyone in your household is missing or has been in New York recently."

Brett began to sweat profusely. He didn't know how to respond. Should he tell the truth and bring the police in or should he keep quiet and try to handle it by himself. "Can you tell me if someone has been killed?" he asked.

"Doctor, I asked you a simple question, are you going to answer it?"

Brett knew someone had been killed. Why else would the homicide division be calling? It couldn't be Annie he thought; why would the kidnappers kill her? She was their ticket to $2 million. Then again, the police were calling him. Maybe something had gone terribly wrong. "Why are you calling me of all people?" He asked, trying to contain the tremble in his voice.

"Doctor, is your wife at home? I'd like to talk to her."

"Well, no she's not. Why do you want to talk to her?"

Doctor Raven, does your wife use Walgreens to fill her prescriptions?"

"Yes, why?"

"We found a pill bottle at a crime scene that we think may have belonged to your wife. Is she missing?"

"No, no, she's not missing."

"I'm going to give you my personal cell phone number. I want to hear from your wife within twenty-four hours or I'm going to assume you're lying to me."

"Sure, give me the number, I'll make certain she calls."

"By the way doctor, have you ever heard the name Stovepipe Wells?'

Brett could barely speak, his mouth had gone dry. Finally, he said, "No, should I?"

"I'll wait for your wife's call," Al said, and hung up the phone and turned to O'Hara. "I'm pretty sure I've found our third hotel guest," he said. "A woman named Annie Raven."

Chapter Six

6 months earlier...

The driver of the parked BMW 321i watched Biff leave the house. He wasn't wearing the game face he had on when he entered it two hours ago, instead he was grinning and had a spring in his step as he approached his rented Tahoe.

Biff pulled away from the curb without even looking into his rear view mirror. The car on the other side of the street made a quick U-turn and fell in thirty yards behind him. A sign, **I 95 South – Miami 68 miles**, came into view and Biff took the forty-five degree jog to the right to enter the freeway while the BMW dropped back to keep a hundred yard separation between the two vehicles.

Traveling at 70 mph it took less than an hour before signs began appearing for the Miami International Airport. Biff exited onto State Road

112 and navigated the Tahoe to the Hertz parking lot. The BMW pulled to the curb ten yards from the driveway.

Fifteen minutes later Biff exited the Hertz office with his overnight case and an envelope that he folded up and stuffed into his back pants pocket before taking a seat on a bench near the driveway. Twenty-five minutes passed before Biff, looking noticeably annoyed, checked his watch. Almost on cue, a Holiday Inn van turned into the driveway and stopped in front of the bench and Biff got in.

The BMW fell into line behind the van and followed it for nine blocks where it turned into the hotel driveway near NW 36th St. Biff, the only passenger in the van, jumped out and handed a dollar to the driver before entering the lobby.

The driver of the BMW waited fifteen minutes and then entered the lobby and headed straight to the front desk. "May I help you?" The clerk asked.

A ten dollar bill quickly appeared on the counter top. "I was hoping to surprise a good friend of mine. He probably checked in this afternoon, Biff Erskine."

The clerk pushed a couple keys on his keyboard as he looked at the computer screen. "I have an Elmer Erskine," he said.

"Oh yes, that's him."

The clerk smiled. "He's in room 321, elevator's

just behind the lobby."

"Thanks."

"My pleasure," the clerk said, as he stuffed the bill into his pocket.

Biff heard a knock on his door. "Who is it?" He asked.

"Mr. Erskine, I need to talk to you."

Biff grabbed his Beretta from the top drawer of the dresser and tucked it into his belt holster just above his buttocks. He cautiously opened the door a crack where he found himself looking at beautiful blonde woman with a 'lights out' figure. "Help you?" he asked.

"I'm Maria, Tony Russo's wife."

"Who's Tony Russo?" Biff asked.

"You know the guy you were talking to this afternoon, J.T. Talbot. I'm not sure right now what his real name is. Can I come in?"

Biff opened the door all the way and gestured to the lone chair in the room. "Can I get you something from the mini bar?" he asked, as Maria sat down on the green Naugahyde vinyl cushion.

"Got a Scotch in there?" Maria asked.

Biff looked in the fridge. "How about a Dewars White Label?"

"That's fine."

He unwrapped two plastic glasses that had been sealed in cellophane and emptied three miniatures from the mini bar into them. "Ice?" he asked.

"A cube is fine."

Biff set Maria's glass next to her on a little round table that had a lamp permanently attached to the top of it. He sat on the end of the bed. "I thought you flew the coop," he said.

"I did," she replied, as she took a taste of Scotch between her lips.

"How did you know I was here?"

"I followed you from the house in West Palm."

"Why?" he asked

"I watched you go in and expected you to bring Ton.., J.T. out in cuffs or something. I was surprised when you came out alone. I figured you cut a deal with him."

"What business is that of yours?"

"I'm prepared to offer you a better one."

Biff sat quietly drinking his liquor and sizing up Maria. What was her game, he was thinking. "What's your deal?" he asked.

Maria set her glass back on the plastic table. "First tell me what he's up to and what he offered you."

Biff was skeptical. "Why should I trust you?"

Maria flashed a wide smile exposing perfectly aligned, pearly white teeth. "Money," she said.

"How much money?"

"Twenty percent more than he's giving you."

"How you goin' to do that?"

Maria picked up her drink and took another sip. "Tell me the deal."

Biff did the math. J.T. was giving him 50% of the kidnap money, $1 million. If Maria was legit, he would get $1.2 million. "He's going to kidnap Brett Raven's wife and demand $2 million for her release."

Maria was silent for a minute while doing her math. "Okay, I'll give you an extra $2 hundred thousand."

"I don't get it, how do you even fit into the deal?"

Maria scooted her chair closer to Biff. "You and J.T. do the dirty work. I'll make sure he's cut out from the payoff. We split the two million, sixty forty. You get the sixty percent."

"How are you going to cut him out?"

Maria inched close enough for Biff to smell her perfume. "That's how I'm going to earn my forty percent. You don't have to know the details as long as I deliver." She gently touched her right hand to his thigh, "Deal?" She asked.

Whether he believed her or was just taken by her charms, he replied, "Deal."

Chapter Seven

San Carlos, Ca.
August 29, 2001

Ginger cancelled most of Brett's patients for the day; however, she left him a voice message telling him she couldn't re-schedule his nine o'clock. He slipped into the building a little after eight and signaled Ginger to meet him in his private office. She joined him in five minutes with two cups of coffee. "How was the flight to the boonies?" she asked.

"All that was there for me was a ransom note."

"Was it from J.T.?"

"Don't know for sure, but I followed a lead and headed to Vegas. The note was given to a delivery pilot by that private investigator from the insurance companies, that big guy Biff."

"Isn't that the guy that you had your gangster friends scare the crap out of?"

"Yeah, but I called him after we recovered the

insurance money and told him he could go after J.T. for the $100 thousand reward. I'm wondering if he's changed uniforms."

Ginger looked perplexed. "Why would he do that?"

"He was hoping to get a big bonus from the insurance companies for recovering the money, but we beat him to it. Maybe he thinks he'll collect from me instead."

"What are you going to do?"

"I need help, I know that for sure. I'm going to call Enrique and Manny."

Ginger rolled her eyes. "Why do you keep going back to those guys? She asked. "Aren't they just small time hoods?"

"Ginger, they're my friends. They came through for me when I needed them to scam the money back from J.T. and they even chipped in a hundred thousand of their cut to pay for the surrogate who's carrying the babies."

"Okay, I get it, I get it, but how can they help you with this?"

"I'm not sure, but they're pretty smart guys and they'll have some ideas."

"Keep me in the loop," Ginger said, as she headed for the door. "Your patient should be here soon, I'm going to the front desk."

"As usual, thanks, Ginger."

"For what?"

"For listening."

Brett took out his cell phone and found the number on his speed dial. "Enrique," the voice answered.

"Hey buddy, it's me."

"Brett, where you been? Haven't heard from you in a month."

"Sorry, I've been swamped. Something really important has come up though, can we talk?"

"Come on down to my office, I'll be here all morning."

"Manny there?"

"You want him here?"

"I think so."

"He'll be here then."

"Thanks, I'll be there about ten-thirty," Brett said and hung up.

Brett smiled as he crossed the railroad tracks into Redwood City and pulled up in front of Enrique's office, a bar in the Mexican section flashing a red neon OPEN sign. He never would have dreamed these men would be his closest friends. He parked his Lexus right in front of the entry door and walked in where he was met by another friend, a huge ugly man with tattoos up and down his thick arms. "Doc," Omar the bodyguard said as he hugged him. "How ya been?"

Brett gave him a pat on the shoulder. "Unfortunately, not so good. I got a big problem and hope the guys can help me out."

"Sorry," Omar replied. "Hope they can. They're waiting for you in the back booth."

Brett slid into the booth next to Manny and across from Enrique. "Thanks for making time," Brett said.

"You kidding? We'll always have time for you. What's up?"

Omar brought three Dos Equis and set them on the table. Brett took a slug and set the bottle back down. "Annie's been kidnapped," he said.

Enrique didn't look surprised. "J.T. or Biff?" he asked.

"Not sure, maybe both."

"How much d' they want?"

"Two million in cash."

"You have it?"

"I could probably drain and borrow to come up with it, but it would destroy the life Annie and I are planning for when the babies arrive."

"Have they given you a drop point or a date?" Manny asked.

"They said seven days to come up with the money."

Enrique was silent, his brain methodically working. Finally he said, "Brett, let me make a couple calls, we still have six days, there may be a way."

"What way?" Brett asked.

"Gimme three days and meet us here at noon. I'll let you know then."

Brett got up to leave. "Thanks, guys, it seems like I'm always asking for favors."

Both Enrique and Manny slid out of the booth and Enrique gave Brett a hug. "Friends, that's what they're for."

"Thanks again, see you day after tomorrow," Brett said, as he made his way toward the door.

Chapter Eight

West Palm Beach, Fla.
February 25, 2001

6 months earlier...

J. T. had two hurdles to jump before the kidnap could take place. He needed to make sure Brett had the money to pay the ransom and he had to latch onto some personal information that would keep Brett from going to the police.

J.T. was Brett's financial advisor for five years before Brett and Annie's divorce. He personally set up Brett's pension plan and advised him that as the trustee, Brett was required to purchase an ERISA Pension Bond. The purpose was to protect the other employees of his professional corporation retirement plan from errors he might make while controlling and investing the funds.

The bond was purchased through Global Surety Bonds Inc. based in Washington D.C. J.T. dialed their number. A receptionist fielded the call,

"Global Bonds."

"Hi, this is Dr. Raven out in California. I have a pension bond with you and I want to make sure it's up to date."

"Hold on, doctor, I'll transfer you to Mark Jenkins."

"Hello doctor, this is Mark, I have your account information in front of me."

"Great, can you tell me how much I'm bonded for?"

"No problem, your policy is for $50,000."

"Wow, I have a lot more than that in my plan."

"Remember doctor, you only have to insure the amount designated for your employees. The government doesn't care if you lose your own share. Last December you reported your pension plan was valued at $850,000 and a liability to your vested employees of only $46,000, so the policy you have looks fine."

J.T. jotted the figure $800,000 on the yellow pad he had in front of him. "Thanks, Mark, it all makes sense now."

"Glad to help, doctor," Mark said and hung up.

J.T. still had work to do. He called the Coldwell Banker real estate office in San Carlos, CA. and was routed to Mary Quinn, an associate realtor. "Hi Mary, my name is Henry Ratcliff. I'm interested in finding a townhouse up the hill off Club Drive. Are there any for sale?"

"Let me look at the listings," she replied. "There isn't anything available right now. How about another area?"

"I don't think so; my wife has her heart set on that location. By the way, what was the price of the last sale up there?"

"Looks like $925,000. Can I call you if something comes up?"

"Sure," J.T. said, and proceeded to give her a phony number. He wrote $900,000 on his pad.

J.T. wasn't sure how to get the last number for his calculation. He popped the top off a Coors Lite and sat back giving it some thought. Finally he went to his computer and found the name and number of a Dental supply company in the San Francisco area. A male voice answered, "Bay View Dental, this is Ted."

"Hello Ted, my name is Jim Carter; I'm a senior dental student at UCSF Dental School."

"What can I do for you doctor?" Ted asked, smelling a prospective sale while patronizing the caller.

"Not a doctor yet, but hopefully in June," J.T. said.

"Well, Jim, what can I do for an almost doctor?"

"I looked at a practice with state of the art equipment, and the seller told me there was a half million dollars of value just in the equipment and furnishings. Does that sound realistic?"

"How many treatment rooms?"

"Six, plus the office stuff and furniture."

"Well it's pretty hard to value without actually appraising it, but if it's almost new I'd make a ballpark guess that it would be worth about $300 thousand tops."

"Wow, if I get serious about it, I better let you appraise it properly?"

"Be my pleasure, Jim. You have my number."

"I'll call you back."

"Thanks for thinking of us."

J.T. was happy. When he added up his figures he was right at $2 million.

The financial part was the easiest hurdle, now he needed to find a weak spot in Brett or Annie's life which could be used as leverage against them. J.T. took out the business card Biff left with him and dialed his number. "Erskine," the voice answered.

"Hey partner, it's time for you to do a little work."

"I've been wondering when you'd call. What's up?"

"I need to know what Brett and Annie have going on in their life. Ever stolen any garbage before?”

Biff broke out in laughter. “I tried that once before with Raven when I was trying to track you. He spotted me and put my dick through a ringer.”

“Well, I guess you’d better be more careful this time; besides, he has no idea what we’re planning so his guard will be down. Collect all their paper stuff and then sift through it for any clue that might indicate what’s big in their life.”

“What are you looking for, exactly?”

“I need something we can threaten them with; something that will force them to go along with us and not call the cops.”

“I’m still not sure what I’m looking for.”

“Biff, it’s hard to explain. Kind of like pornography, I can’t define it, but I know it when I see it. Just get me some stuff, I can’t tell you what exactly, but I’ll recognize it when you come up with it.”

“So, you lookin’ for some dirt?”

J.T. rolled his eyes. “No, I didn’t mean that. Forget the porn analogy, just sift through everything. You’re a private dick, you’ll be able to recognize unusual stuff.”

Biff sounded worried. “What if I don’t come up with anything?”

“This is worth a million dollars to you Biff, you’ll find something.”

"When do you need it?"

"Take your time. Garbage is a once a week exercise, so take a month if you need to."

Chapter Nine

When Biff previously sifted through Brett and Annie's garbage he'd been careless. He had no idea they had discovered him, and they set him up by planting phony documents along with the other papers they had thrown out. This time he would be more careful.

The garbage cans were put out Thursday night for pickup early Friday morning. The mistake Biff previously made was to sift through the cans while right next to the garage, before the garbage collectors arrived. This Friday morning, he was parked on the main street, out of sight from Geranium Lane, the cul-de-sac on which the Ravens lived.

It was four thirty-five a.m. when the garbage trucks arrived and stopped on Club Drive, adjacent to the cul-de-sac. Two burly guys dressed in jeans, tee shirts, and leather gloves jumped off the rear of the truck and started toward the townhouses. Biff intercepted them. "Hey guys," he yelled.

The biggest of the two turned, displaying a set of oversized biceps, and said to Biff, "You talkin' to us?"

"Yeah, you guys interested in making a couple hundred extra bucks?"

"Like how?" the shorter guy asked.

Biff stepped closer flashing a stolen police detective badge for which he had paid two hundred dollars in a pawn shop. Handing the guys a box of large plastic garbage bags he said, "When you dump the recycle shit from #44, put it in one of these bags. I'll give you a hundred every week for the bag."

"No problem" the big man said and grabbed the bags.

Two minutes later the garbage collectors dropped a bulging sack at Biff's feet. He picked it up and handed them a crisp hundred dollar bill. "Thanks, guys, see ya next Friday," he said, and headed for his car.

When Biff got back to his apartment, he emptied the garbage bag of papers into a pile on his rug. Some of them were shredded and others were torn in half or wadded up. He put the shreds back into the plastic bag, flattened out the others, and began piecing them together. Most of the collection was advertisements or junk mail, but one piece of paper had the look of something official. It had been torn into about eight pieces and Biff was able to recover four of them. He pieced together what he had and put tape over the edges.

The partial letterhead read *LGT... 450 Sutte... Franci..CA.* He couldn't make out the phone number but he did have part of the text. *...appoint... ... onday, ... 20th ... o'clock...* Biff carefully set the fragment into a manila folder.

The garbage the following week was totally fruitless: a pile of store catalogs, a couple flyers for free chiropractic exams, and a bunch of torn up solicitation letters.

The third week looked like it would be a carbon copy of the previous one until Biff spotted a partial return address on a torn up envelope - *LGTI.* He couldn't find the rest of the envelope so he set the piece he had into his folder.

Biff slipped the garbage guys their fourth hundred dollar bill and headed back to his apartment with a bulging plastic bag. As usual he dumped the contents onto his rug, spread it out, and began sifting through it. "Same old shit," he muttered.

Most of the fragments had been picked up and put back in the bag when he spotted a familiar letterhead, *LGTI*.   He rummaged through the remaining papers but couldn't find pieces that might match the letter, so he dumped the bag out again and started through it a second time.

This time he spotted several fragments he missed on the first go around. One contained a partial sentence ... *Samantha ...... delighted...* another, *twins....* and a final one, *projected d... date, ...ct. 16 th...* Biff put the pieces into his folder and picked up the phone.

The call was answered on the first ring. "Antonio here."

"J.T. cut the phony name bullshit, this is Biff."

"What's up? Have something?"

"I think so. Should I send it or fax it."

"FedEx it overnight. You have my address."

"Will do," Biff said, and hung up.

West Palm Beach, Fla.

April 2, 2001

The FedEx truck arrived the next afternoon and after signing for it, J.T. took the envelope into his office and began decoding the contents. He came up with: *LGTI, 450 Sutter St. San Francisco, CA. appointment Monday, Samantha delighted, twins, projected due date.*

He went quickly to his computer and opened up Google, a new search engine he recently heard about. He typed in LGTI. A webpage popped up.

LGTI—Life's Greatest Treasure Institute
450 Sutter, San Francisco, California.
415-555-1200
A private institute dedicated to providing a surrogate to any woman who wishes to have a baby, but cannot carry a fetus in her own body.

He smiled to himself as he turned off his computer. Annie was pregnant in 1995, had a miscarriage and was told she should never get pregnant again. That had led to her divorce from Brett.

J.T. dialed Biff's number. "Erskine here," the voice answered.

"Biff, J.T., got a minute?"

"Let me check my calendar, I've been swamped lately." Without hesitation he said, "Luckily, I'm free for a couple months."

"I've got another assignment for you." J.T. said.

Chapter Ten

San Francisco, Ca.
April 5, 2001

Biff looked at the directory in the lobby of the 450 Sutter building. **LGTI**, *Life's Greatest Treasure Institute*, was located on the 14th floor. J.T. had given him specific instructions: case the place first, come back after hours for the information.

A security guard was stationed near the elevator as Biff approached. "Do the doc's work late in this building? I may need evening appointments," Biff asked.

The uniformed, gray haired old man, looking as if he had just awakened from a deep sleep, looked lazily at Biff, "Some do, some don't. If you come in after seven-thirty, you have to sign in though. One shrink has patients coming in as late as eleven, but he's nuttier than they are."

"Thanks," Biff said. "This elevator go up to the 21st floor?"

"Yup, just takes a while."

Biff got off at fourteen and spotted the door immediately. "Good morning; may I help you?" the receptionist asked.

Biff had put on his only tie under his seven year old blue blazer, rubbed some hair gel into his crew cut, and taken the time for a close shave; he looked respectable. "I hope so," he said, while casually looking beyond the reception desk. "My wife and I are thinking of utilizing your services. Do you have any brochures or stuff like that?"

The smartly dressed young lady jumped to her feet. "Certainly, let me run and get you our introductory package," she said, as she disappeared behind a partition.

Biff began making mental notes. There didn't appear to be any alarms or cameras. Most likely no money was kept in the office so they relied on the 'Rent-A-Cop' stationed on the first floor for their security. Three feet behind the reception desk were four floor to ceiling metal filing cabinets, which he assumed contained what he was looking for.

"Here you are," the receptionist said, as she returned and handed Biff a large packet with a multicolored cover displaying a mother and father holding a newborn. "Would you like to talk to one of our counselors?'

"Not yet. Let my wife and I look this over, and

we'll make an appointment if we think it's for us."

The young lady smiled, "Call us anytime between eight-thirty and five-thirty."

Biff returned to the lobby at 8:45 p.m. and once again looked over the directory. "Help ya?" the evening security uniform asked.

Biff walked over to him and whispered, "I've got an appointment with a psychiatrist, Dr. Winslow. What floor is he on?"

"Oh, the doc with the late appointments. He's on twelve, just sign this register."

"Thanks," Biff replied, as he signed a phony name in the book and got into the elevator. Just in case the guard was watching the elevator lights, he pushed twelve, got out there, and used the stairs to get up to fourteen. He took a little leather pouch out of his pocket and fished through it for the proper tools. He chose three little picks and teased them one at a time into the lock until he heard a click; he turned the knob and the door opened.

The office was dark. Biff lit up a small flashlight that he pulled from his jacket pocket and aimed the beam toward the floor as he walked to the file cabinets. Upon closer examination he realized the cabinets were separated alphabetically; he opened the one that read P-Z. He quickly went to the R's and spotted a file labeled Raven. He pulled it out, laid it on the reception desk and opened it. There were over fifty papers in the file, but J.T. was specific about what he wanted. About two-thirds through the stack he found what he was looking for, the name and address of the surrogate carrying the Raven babies. He jotted the information on a mini-notebook he carried in with him.

Samantha O'Brian
2474 9th Avenue
San Francisco, Ca.

Biff replaced the file, locked the office and walked down to the twelfth floor. He waited a half hour and at 9:45 took the elevator back to the lobby, thanked the security guard, and left the 450 Sutter building.

He dusted off his 35 mm Minolta, twisted on a telephoto lens, loaded it with a fresh roll of film, and set it on the car seat next to him. By 8:00 a.m. he was parked on 9th Ave. across from 2474 keeping an eye on the front door. Around 8:30 a young man in his early thirties walked out and headed toward the streetcar stop a half block away. The door didn't open again until 9:45 when a plain looking young lady wearing maternity clothes came out and locked it behind her. Biff adjusted the telephoto lens and began clicking the shutter on his Minolta. He made sure he took many facial shots and also close-ups of her swollen belly.

CHAPTER ELEVEN

San Francisco, Ca.
June 5, 2001

Samantha loved being pregnant. She had three kids of her own and had been a surrogate once before. When Brett and Annie chose her to carry the embryos which were produced from their eggs and sperm, she was ecstatic. Four embryos had been planted in her uterus and two of them had survived. She was carrying twins.

Tonight was the celebration dinner. Annie reserved a quiet table at the Boulevard restaurant in San Francisco on Mission Street near the Embarcadero and she and Brett made sure to arrive twenty minutes before Samantha and her husband. "Two Tanquery martinis, up, dry and olives on the side," Brett said to the waiter. "Oh, and also a bottle of Rombauer Chardonnay."

"A bit surreal, isn't it?" Annie said, after the drinks arrived.

"It really is. Not too many parents can have dinner with the person who's carrying their babies. When is the official birth date?"

"She's almost five months right now, so the doctor figures October 16th."

"Still can't believe it."

Before Annie could respond she spotted their guests coming toward the table. Samantha was thirty-one years old, very plain looking, wore no makeup, and was dressed in a loose fitting print dress that draped over her protruding belly. Following close behind, thin and about six feet tall, dressed in khakis and a floral sport shirt was her husband, who was repeatedly looking at his wrist watch as if he had a more important meeting to attend than this one.

Brett and Annie jumped to their feet to greet the couple, and Annie thrust her arms around Samantha. "You look wonderful. How do you feel?"

"I feel great, just great. This is my husband Todd." Brett threw him a strong handshake, but received a 'wet fish' in return. Everyone took seats at the table.

Annie sensed Todd's discomfort and immediately turned the conversation toward him. "Samantha said you were in grad school."

"Yes," he said, averting eye contact. "I'm working on my masters in psychology."

"That's where the surrogacy money is going," Samantha added.

"When will you finish up?" Annie asked.

"One more year for my masters," Todd replied, taking a second gulp of the Chardonnay that the waiter had poured from the bottle already on the table. "Another two for the doctorate," he added, with a note of pride and another gulp of wine.

"That sounds great," Brett said. "With all the drama in our life we'll be ready for a psychologist by then. You can schedule us as your first patients."

Todd laughed and drained the wine from his glass, "That's a deal."

Annie turned to Samantha. "Is there anything you need?' she asked.

"Not really, the agency supplies almost everything from the fees you guys paid. I want to thank both of you again for choosing me to be a part of this with you."

Both Brett and Annie responded at once. "It's we who thank you."

While everyone looked at the menus, Annie got things started with an appetizer of Monterey Red Abalone. They eventually decided on splitting a couple Fuji apple bleu cheese salads; Samantha and Todd went for the red meat main courses, while Annie and Brett opted for fish.

I'm stuffed," Todd said, as they finished their

toasted Pecan Cake dessert. He looked at his watch for the first time since sitting down. "I can't believe it's ten-thirty."

Brett pushed his chair away from the table, signaling an end to the pleasant evening. Feeling the wine and finally feeling at ease Todd said, "It was wonderful meeting you both. Sam told me you were great people and she was right. Thanks for the lovely dinner." To everyone's surprise, he gave Brett a hug and kissed Annie on the cheek.

"Don't worry about your twins," Samantha said, patting her stomach. "I'm taking good care of them."

Brett merged onto highway 101 and headed south toward San Carlos. Neither spoke until Annie said, "I just want her to be safe."

"Why wouldn't she be?" Brett rhetorically asked.

Chapter Twelve

San Francisco, Ca.
July 20, 2001

The sun was out almost everywhere in California except here, where the fog was rolling in over the hills and spreading its tentacles across the downtown area like an octopus looking for prey. It was a typical summer day in San Francisco.

Biff always wondered why he had made this city his home; the views were beautiful, but the weather was lousy, and lousy weather depressed him. Today was especially bad; all he could see from his window was gray mist that was condensing on the glass and forming droplets that were running to the bottom of the frame.

He had other reasons to be depressed besides the weather. It had been a month since he had heard anything from his partner J.T. and a couple months since his meeting with his supposed partner Maria. Biff pulled up both numbers on his cell phone.

"Leave a message," was all J.T.'s machine said.

"Uh, J.T., this is Biff, what's happening? I haven't heard from you since I sent all that stuff to you six weeks ago. I passed up a 100 K for not bringing you in, you owe me a call."

Biff hadn't eaten all day and went to the fridge hoping there was still something there worth eating. He was disappointed; an open package of bologna had turned brown and a partially eaten hunk of cheese was bordering on green. "Shit," he said, as he heaved them into the garbage. He settled for one of his last two cans of Keystone.

By the time he was finishing the second can his phone rang. "Yeah, Biff," he answered.

"Biff, it's me J.T."

"Where you been? I was afraid you skipped on me."

"Sorry," J.T. replied. "I should have called."

"We still on?"

"You bet. I've worked out most of the details. Is this phone safe?"

"Should be, I haven't done anything illegal. Yet!"

"Okay, here's how it's going down. I'll make the trip to San Francisco and get Annie. You'll head out to Las Vegas and arrange to deliver the ransom note. We'll meet back in New York City a day later. I've arranged for a suite in a small hotel where we can headquarter until Raven flies out there with the money."

"New York, why the hell New York?"

"We have to get him out of his comfort zone. If we do the deal in California he'll have a step up on us. I know he's never been to New York and I have, and I know the city real well. I want to be in control and there I will be."

Biff was mentally counting the dollars in his bank account. "Who's paying for the plane tickets and the hotel?"

"I'll put up the money and take it off the top before we split the ransom. A week before we're ready to go, I'll send you the note along with instructions and a couple tickets."

"A week before when? When's this happening?"

"August, it's going to happen the end of August."

"Why so long?" Biff asked, still worrying about stretching his bank account for two months.

"Our leverage is that woman whose carrying Annie and Brett's future twins, and I want to make sure the babies are close to term. A threat to them is our insurance for cooperation."

Biff had no choice but to go along. "Okay, but keep in touch, I don't like being left in the dark."

"Of course, sorry about that." J.T. said, apologetically.

"All right I'll wait to hear from you, and by the

way, send me a thousand bucks as an advance on my cut."

There was a pause and then J.T. replied. "No problem, I'll drop it in the mail tomorrow."

As soon as he hung up from J.T. Biff dialed the number Maria had given him. Her simple "hello" conjured up the image of her gorgeous face and perfect body.

"Maria, this is Biff, remember me?"

"What kind of a question is that?" she replied.

"I haven't heard from you."

"Biff, you're the one to keep me informed, not the other way around. What's happening?"

"It's going down in August. Our deal is for you to get J.T. out of the way somehow and we split the money. You figure out how?"

"You don't have to remind me what our deal is, and don't worry, I'll keep my end of the bargain. What do you know so far?"

"J.T. has leverage on Raven and his wife to persuade them to go along. He's going to take her to New York."

"Did you say New York?" Maria asked incredulously.

"That's what he said. Thinks he'll have the upper hand there. I don't really give a shit as long as he delivers."

"You're right; it's no different for us. Call me

one week before it happens."

"Okay, this number?'

"Yes, and Biff?"

"What?"

"Do you still have that gun you were flashing at the motel in Miami?"

"Yeah, I still have it, why?" Biff asked.

"Does it have a silencer?"

"Yeah, but why…?"

"Can you file the serial numbers off it?"

"Sure, but I didn't plan on…."

"Look Biff, this is hardball. You want to be in the game or not?"

"Yeah, I do, but I'm not goin' to kill anyone."

"Just bring the gun and make sure it can't be traced. You won't have to kill him." Biff was silent, while his brain processed this new development. "Biff, are you in, or is this too much for an ex-marine?" Maria asked, sarcastically.

He regained his composure. "I'm in, I'm in. I'll bring the weapon."

"That's more like it," Maria said. "I'll wait for your call."

Chapter Thirteen

San Carlos, Ca.
August 27, 2001

Brett left for the office an hour and twenty minutes ago and Annie was getting ready for a quick trip up to San Francisco for lunch with Samantha when she heard an abrupt knock on the front door of the townhouse. "Who is it?" she yelled, but there was no answer. "Damn," she muttered to herself, anticipating a late start to the city.

She set her coffee cup in the sink and went to the door. Thinking it must be her next door neighbor, she said, "That you, Pam?" as she opened the door. All the blood drained from her face and she could feel a shivering adrenalin response which set her hands shaking like tree limbs in a heavy wind.

"Hello, Annie, how's my ex-wife doing?" the man said.

Annie had only seen J.T. once since his supposed

death in a plane crash a year and a half ago. That was in West Palm Beach, Florida, when he had spotted her and chased her car; she had narrowly escaped. "What the hell are you doing here?" she said defiantly.

"May I come in?" J.T. asked.

"No way! What do you want?"

"What would you think if I said I'm here to get back some of my $5 million you and Brett conned me into losing."

Annie smirked, "That wasn't your money, it belonged to the insurance companies you swindled."

"Why did you do it?" J.T. asked.

"Do what?"

"I left you a $5 million life insurance policy. You could have kept the money and still re-married Brett and you'd be on 'Easy Street.' Instead, you guys give the money back and trick me into doing the same. Why, I don't get it."

"That's the difference between you and us. We have ethics and morals, you have neither. You went from a respected financial counselor to a crook." She was beginning to hyperventilate and was feeling a little dizzy. "I'll ask you again, what are you doing here?"

"You don't look well, we better talk inside."

Annie knew she should end this right away. She stepped back and slammed the door as hard as she could, but J.T. put the sole of his shoe next to the jamb. He pushed the door back open, walked inside, and closed it behind him. Annie ran to the kitchen, grabbed the wall phone and managed to push 9-1-1 before J.T. shoved her out of the way, disconnected the call, and hung the receiver back on the cradle. He pointed his finger at her and said, "The phone is going to ring and I'm going to pick it up. Don't you say a word."

"Or what? You going to kill me?"

"I don't have to. If you utter a sound, Samantha and your babies will pay the price."

Annie was petrified. What did that mean? He knows about Samantha?

The phone rang. "Hello," J.T. answered.

"This is the San Carlos Police department. Did you just call 911?"

"I'm afraid we did, sorry. Our alarm sets the call off if we're late with our code. I thought we got to it in time."

"May I have your name sir?"

"Raven, Doctor Brett Raven."

There was a pause while the dispatcher checked a cross reference. "Thank you, sir, next time try to get that code in faster."

"I will, thank you for following up so fast," J.T. said, as he hung up the receiver.

Annie's knees were knocking against each

other. "What, what did you mean, my babies will pay the price?"

He took an envelope out of his pocket, handed it to her, and watched her face blanch as she thumbed through its contents: a dozen close up photos of Samantha's face and swollen abdomen. "You're going to come with me to catch a plane at eleven forty-five. If you resist or try to tip anyone off, she'll get a baseball bat in her belly compliments of my partner. I can't begin to imagine what that would do to those sweet little guys in there."

Annie's jaw fell open. "You were always selfish, but when I married you, you weren't the monster I'm seeing now."

"Circumstances shape the person. I'm desperate, Annie, I'm very desperate. Now let's go to your bedroom and pack your suitcase. You may be away for a while."

J.T. followed Annie upstairs. She pulled a suitcase off the top shelf of the closet, began opening drawers and threw clothes and cosmetics haphazardly into the leather valise. "Don't look so surprised," J.T. said. "Did you really expect that I would just kiss off $5 million without retaliating?"

"Brett has friends who won't be happy with this when they find out. You may end up with a bullet in your head."

"I'll risk it. Hurry it up we have a plane to

catch."

J.T. carried the suitcase down the stairs and to the front door. "Take off that necklace," he ordered.

Annie handed it to him. He removed the gold heart, put it in his pocket, and left the chain on the front hall table. He slammed the door behind them.

Chapter Fourteen

Millbrae, Ca.
August 27, 2001

Annie scrutinized J.T. as he drove toward the San Francisco airport. He told her he was desperate and his look and demeanor appeared to support that statement. Throughout the eleven years she had known him, including the five they were married, he was always well groomed, wore the best clothes and displayed an air of confidence; not so today.

He was overdue for a haircut; his blond hair was beginning to curl at the base of his neck and around his ears. It looked as if he hadn't shaved in two or three days and stubble was forming on his cheeks, chin and neck. Annie was sure the clothes he had on were the same he had worn on the plane to San Francisco. The khakis were wrinkled with a tear where the pocket attached, and his light blue shirt had a huge spot on the front where a hunk of greasy food must have dropped on it.

Annie had always marveled at the way J.T. could keep his emotions hidden in a crisis and could always project an aura of calm. As she now zeroed in on his facial expression, she immediately noticed a slight tic in his left eye that had never been there previously, and his movements were jerky as opposed to the smooth and fluid grace he once displayed.

This man, who she once thought she was in love with, now scared the hell out of her. Was he really capable of violence? "Do you think you'll actually get away with this?" Annie asked.

"Why wouldn't I?" he responded. "I know Brett; he'll do anything to keep you and your babies safe, and he's smart enough and arrogant enough not to bring the police into it. Besides, he doesn't want to stir the hornet's nest he stumbled into last year. He knows he'll get bitten this time."

"Who's your partner in this? You can't pull it off by yourself."

His right eye twitched twice involuntarily. "You know what Annie? Why don't you shut the fuck up. When I want conversation, I'll ask for it."

"Aren't you a little ashamed of yourself? The straight 'A' student from Stanford, the respected professional financial planner has ended up a kidnapper and a criminal."

J.T. turned toward Annie and swung the back of his right hand across her left cheek. "I said, "Shut the fuck up."

Annie could taste blood in her mouth, oozing from her upper lip, which had been cut by being forced against her central incisors. She sucked it into her saliva, turned to her left, and spit. The pale pink mixture splattered against J.T.'s cheek and dripped down onto his shirt creating a bulls-eye on the already existing stain. "You son of a bitch, what makes you think I'll go along with this?" She said defiantly.

J.T. took a Kleenex from his pocket, wiped his face and shirt, and threw it on the floor.

"You want to know who my partner is? Okay, it's Biff Erskine, the guy Brett sent to take me back to face insurance fraud charges. That guy hates your husband more than I do. I'd worry about him before you worry about me. He wouldn't hesitate for a minute to harm your surrogate Samantha, especially when a couple million dollars are at stake."

Annie wiped her lip with the back of her hand and dried it on her jeans. "Brett doesn't have that kind of money," she said.

"He'll get it. I may not like him, but I know he's a smart guy. He'll get the money, trust me, he will." J.T. pulled into the Hertz return lot. "We're getting on the shuttle bus and then the airplane. Biff is in San Francisco right now." He took out his cell phone. "I have his number on speed dial. If you shout out or bolt, I hit number three right here, and you'll be the one responsible for the abortion of those twins."

Abortion, there was that word again. It made her shiver. Annie became pregnant when she and Brett were living together in their sophomore year at Berkeley. She wanted to keep the baby, but Brett pressured her to terminate the pregnancy and now she can't become pregnant.

"They're going to come after you, you know" she said.

"Who?" J.T. asked.

"Brett's friends, Enrique and Manny, the guys who conned you out of the $5.5 million of stolen money."

"Those chicken shit bastards, I'm looking forward to meeting them again."

"You always were a big talker, but talk won't help you. Those guys will chew you up and spit you out like a lion getting rid of bones."

"I'm counting on Biff to keep that from happening. He has a score to settle with those guys just like I do. He never goes anywhere without his pistol and he'll have no problem using it if we meet up with those small time gangsters."

The shuttle pulled up in front of the United terminal. J.T. hit number three on his speed dial and put the phone to Annie's ear. "Hello, Mrs. Raven, this is your old buddy Biff."

"Big brave Biff. You really up to attacking a defenseless woman carrying two babies?"

"That depends on you. Right now I'm in the 450 Sutter building, watching the door of the LGT institute. If you don't get on that plane, you'll find out the answer to your question. Have a nice flight; I heard your ex booked first class." Biff said, and clicked off his cell.

Annie had no choice but to board the flight. She would never forgive herself if she called Biff's hand and found out he wasn't bluffing.

"Welcome," the flight attendant said, as she pointed the duo toward the front section of the aircraft.

J.T. nudged Annie forward. "You take the window seat," he said. She slid in next to the window, and J.T. took up a guard position on the aisle. "If this goes well, you'll be back with Brett in a week and be a proud momma of twins in another month. If not, those babies may never be born, or may be missing a mommy, a daddy, or both." Annie looked away and stared out through the Plexiglas.

The attendant powered the door hatch to the locked position and the airliner began a push back from the gate. "Sit back and enjoy the flight," she said over the PA system. "We'll be landing at Kennedy in New York City in five hours and forty-three minutes."

Chapter Fifteen

New York, N.Y.
August 27, 2001

"Get in," J.T. ordered. Annie did as she was told and slid across the back seat of the Yellow Cab.

"Where you wanna go?" the driver asked, in a Middle Eastern accent.

"Times Square Hotel on 46th, know it?" J.T. asked.

"I know it, but I get you a more better one. Very cheap! My brother, he's the manager."

"Yeah, thanks buddy, but how about just taking us to the Times Square."

"No problem, no problem," the driver said, as he merged into bumper to bumper traffic on the Van Wyck Expressway. Pouting a little, he placed a bud from his phone into his ear and was soon deep in conversation speaking a language which sounded much like Farsi.

"Why so quiet?" J.T. said to Annie.

She looked at him with hatred in her eyes. "What is it with you? I used to think you were one of the smartest guys I'd ever met, but now it appears you're one of the stupidest."

"Why do you say that?"

"Are you kidding me? You're a liar, a bigamist, a kidnapper, and from what I see, a possible baby killer."

His face took on a remorseful expression. "Annie, I'm not a bad person; you lived with me, you must know that."

"Have you looked at yourself lately? You're not the man who was Brett's best friend or the man I turned to when I was struggling with my divorce. You're a narcissistic asshole who only cares about himself and is willing to do anything to gain back what he's lost."

J.T.'s moment of remorse was replaced by anger. "You have no idea what it's like to be on top of the world one day and at the bottom a day later."

"Oh, you poor man, let me feel sorry for you: The man who chose to gamble on investments and lost. The man who married another woman when he was married to me. The man, who faked his own death, collected insurance money and disappeared. Oh, I feel so sorry for you."

"I left you a life insurance policy worth $5

million," he said sheepishly.

Annie looked at him with contempt. "That's your idea of doing the right thing? Just leave me some stolen money and everything will be square. I once admired you, the hard working guy who came from nothing and became a self-made man. Now I pity you, you're nothing more than a common criminal." She crossed her arms on her chest and looked out the side window.

J.T. had no response and his eye began to twitch again. He tried to stop the involuntary movement, but he had no control and eventually he just ignored it. The traffic which had thinned out for a while suddenly came to a stop. "What's the problem?" he asked the driver.

The driver, looking annoyed, took the earpiece out and laid it next to his cell. "What's that?" he asked.

"Why we stopping?"

"Bridge toll. Give me six bucks."

Angry at himself for asking, J.T. opened his wallet and counted out six singles. "It's not included in the fare?"

"Not included," the driver replied, as he grabbed the money and stuffed the bud back in his ear.

Annie continued to stare out the window as the cab made its way into Manhattan and onto 42nd street. It was after 10 p.m. and the mini skirted prostitutes had already taken up residence on the corners where they were blatantly displaying their wares. Turning to J.T. she said, "Nice area you picked. Remind me never to use your travel agent."

His demeanor had changed drastically since getting into the cab at the airport. "Just keep your mouth shut from now on. When we get to the hotel stand beside me and don't say a word. I don't want to call Biff with any bad news."

J.T. gave Annie a little push to get her out of the taxi and then gave the cabbie fifty dollars for the meter plus an extra five. The driver looked at the bills and dumped their two suitcases on the curb while muttering an unintelligible insult under his breath.

J.T. ignored him and nudged Annie toward the front desk; she heard him address the clerk, "Mr. & Mrs. Hansen."

The clerk switched screens on her computer. "Welcome, Mr. Hansen, which credit card will you be using for your stay?"

J.T. reached into his side pocket and took out a wad of bills. "My wallet was stolen yesterday; I'll just pay with cash if that's okay."

"Certainly, cash still works. It looks like you're booked for four nights. The total will be $1,316.88."

J.T. peeled off fourteen hundreds and handed them to the clerk. After counting them she made change and slipped a form in front of him. "Just sign the registration and we're good to go."

"After you, dear," J.T. said, in a voice meant to be heard by the clerk, as he steered Annie toward the folding iron gate of the elevator. "Push five," he said, after he had both suitcases safely tucked inside.

Each floor in the Times Square Hotel had only one suite on it and unlike most of the hotels in big cities, which by now used electronic keys, the Times Square still used old fashioned metal ones. J.T. placed it into the keyhole just below the doorknob of 561, the designated suite for floor five.

J.T. bolted the door lock after they entered and did a quick tour of the room layout. There was an ample sized living room with a TV, fold-out couch, two stuffed chairs, a table with seating for four, and a small kitchenette containing a coffee maker, toaster and microwave. The living room connected with a bedroom to the right and another to the left. Both of the bedrooms had a TV, a good size bathroom, and a shower. "Take your pick," he said. Annie grabbed her suitcase and rammed it against the jamb as she pushed it into the smaller room on the left and slammed the door behind her. She heard a click from the door knob and when she turned it, she realized J.T. had somehow locked it from the other side.

She looked around the room. There was only one window which looked out on an alley five floors below. She tried to open it, but like most hotels in Manhattan, it was bolted shut to keep in the winter heat and summer air conditioning. There were three doors: one to the closet, one to the bathroom, and the locked one to the living room. There was no phone. She sat down on the bed and with a feeling of despair realized she was a prisoner and this room was her cell.

Chapter Sixteen

New York City, N.Y.
August 29, 2001

"I hate New York," Biff said.

"Yeah, then why don't ya go back where you came from," The cab driver replied, giving him the finger.

"See, you're like all the other assholes in this city, always ready to argue about something."

"Hey man, I have to drive you; I don't have to listen to you. If you don't like it here, keep it to yourself. I got my own problems."

"Fine, but open the window so I don't have to smell the B.O. in here. Don't you people ever take a bath?"

"What d'ya mean 'you people'?

"Where you from, India or Pakistan or somewhere like that?"

The driver gave him the finger again. "Close, I'm from the Bronx, right next to Afghanistan."

"You look Indian."

"Yeah, well you look fat."

"Up yours, "Biff said.

"Up yours too," the cabbie answered back.

Biff was tired and put an end to the enlightened conversation until he spied the skyline of Manhattan through the windshield. "Drive straight to the hotel, I don't want you looking lost and running up the meter."

"Don't worry, the sooner I get you out of my cab the better."

The taxi pulled up in front of the Times Square Hotel and Biff jumped out. The driver stayed put and said through the open window, "fifty-five-fifty."

Biff pulled three twenty's from his wallet and handed them to the cabbie. "Keep the change," he said.

The driver looked at the bills and said, "Sure you can spare it?"

"Buy yourself some deodorant, on me," Biff replied, snatching his overnight case and heading for the front door of the hotel.

"What room are the Hansen's in?" Biff asked at the front desk. "I'm staying with them."

The clerk scanned her computer screen. "Number 561, a very nice suite. Elevator's in the rear of the lobby."

Biff was sure the elevator was straining against

his weight, but it delivered him safely to the fifth floor. He spotted the room and knocked. "Who is it?" a voice from inside asked.

"It's me, Biff."

The door opened and J.T. motioned him in. "Good job on the phone with Annie. Any problems delivering the note?" he asked.

"Nah, had a kid fly it over to Stovepipe from Vegas. How about the woman, is she here?"

"Safe and sound," J.T. replied, pointing to the locked bedroom. "Not exactly a happy camper though."

"Hey, I wouldn't be either. Where do I sleep?" Biff asked, looking around and only seeing two bedrooms.

"Since you're the last to show up, you get the fold out couch."

"What about a crapper?"

"Share mine in there," J.T. said, pointing to the bedroom opposite Annie's.

"What about food?"

"We'll order meals in the room or you can get us 'take out.' We'll pay cash; no way we can use credit cards."

Biff nodded his approval. "I'm gonna get a drink at that bar across the street. Want a Scotch to go?"

"No, I'm fine, I brought a flask. You go ahead."

Biff risked his life again with the elevator and

again it proved to be reliable. He pulled a wadded up piece of note paper from his pocket and approached the concierge, an older woman with light blue hair and horned rim glasses who reminded him of Miss Forester, his sixth grade teacher. "How far is this address from here?" he asked.

The matron smiled and looked at the paper. "Oh my, that's the Algonquin Hotel, it's beautiful." She took out a street map and spread it open on her desk. "We're on 46th right here," she said, circling the point on the map with a ball point. "The Algonquin's on 44th," she said, while making another circle. "One block over, two blocks down."

Three blocks of walking had Biff sucking for air as he entered the hotel. The lobby was gorgeous. It had changed its décor since it opened a hundred years ago, but not its elegance. It was lit by crystal chandeliers which were hung from twenty-five foot ceilings and was furnished with red and blue velour over-stuffed chairs and sofas. It reeked of money.

Biff caught sight of his own reflection in the glass door as it revolved away from him. He smoothed the front of his shirt and tucked a wayward flap back into his trousers under his worn out blue blazer. "Could you ring Maria Russo's room, please," he asked the man at the front desk, who in contrast to him, was smartly dressed in a lightweight tan suit, blue shirt and tie.

"Certainly, sir," he replied, in a patronizing manner while evaluating Biff's wardrobe. "Whom may I say is inquiring?"

"John Rockefeller," Biff replied, taking offense to his air of superiority.

The clerk forced a smile and dialed a house phone. "A Mr. Rockefeller to see you Ms. Russo." He placed the phone back in the cradle and said to Biff, "She'll meet you in the cocktail lounge in five minutes."

"Thanks," Biff said, and handed the man a wrinkled dollar bill, that was drenched from being held in his sweaty hand.

She looked even more beautiful than when he had met her back in Miami six months ago. Her long blond hair flowed down her back over a white silk blouse which was tucked into a pair of tight pink Capris. Her open toed high heels clicked on the marble, and her straw shoulder bag swung back and forth as she approached the cocktail table, where Biff was seated nursing a bottle of Bud. "Hello, Mr. Rockefeller," she said, holding her bright red polished nails out in Biff's direction.

Biff shook her hand. "Nice to see ya again, partner. Drink?"

"Vodka Gimlet," she said, to a waiter who had appeared from nowhere. "How was the flight," she asked, making small talk.

"Fine, but your ex wouldn't spring for first, so I

was back in the cattle car."

"How is Tony, or … J.T.? The last time I saw him he was half drunk and blubbering in our townhouse in West Palm."

"He's fine. He holding Raven's wife three blocks from here."

The waiter placed a fancy martini glass in front of Maria and poured her drink into it from a small stainless shaker. After he was gone she said, "Give me the name of the hotel and the room number."

Biff took the pen from the leather folder containing the bar bill and jotted the information on a cocktail napkin. He folded it and handed it to Maria. "When?" he asked.

"Did you bring the pistol?"

He nodded. "In my belt holster."

Maria snatched a large cloth napkin from the empty table next to them. "Wrap it in this and set it next to my purse."

Biff tucked the napkin under his jacket and pulled his Beretta out of the holster with it. He set the package on the table. Maria opened her purse, and as delicately as putting back a tube of lipstick, she slipped the napkin along with the pistol into her shoulder bag and snapped it shut.

"How about the silencer?" she asked.

"Oh yeah." Biff reached in his jacket pocket and took out a felt pouch about six inches long that was cinched tight with a draw string. He handed it to Maria, who deposited it into her bag next to the Berretta . When?" Biff asked again.

"I should have an apartment ready for us very soon. We have to get her out of the hotel right after it's over."

"You better get busy. Raven will be on his way out here with the money in a few days."

"Okay, I'll have everything ready to go by tomorrow afternoon . You're not going to chicken out on me, are you?"

Biff finished off his beer. "I think I'm good with it as long as you pull the trigger."

"Don't worry about that."

"Our deal still the same? I get a million two?"

"Still the same. You're a couple days away from being a rich man," Maria said, as she pushed her chair back from the table.

"What should I do?" Biff asked.

"Annie doesn't eat with you does she?"

"Nah, J.T. has her holed up in a bedroom. There's a table in the living room for us to eat at. Why?"

"I'll knock on the door tomorrow at dinnertime, around six. You open it for me and I'll join you guys at the table. Then just stay out of the way."

Biff blotted a couple beads of sweat from his forehead with a cocktail napkin. "Don't worry, I will."

THE TRAIL

9/1/01 – 9/8/01

CHAPTER SEVENTEEN

Redwood City, Ca.
September 1, 2001

Brett pulled up in front of Enrique's bar, parked in the red zone, and flipped the keys to Omar. "Would you keep an eye out? Move it if the meter maid shows up."

"Sure doc, but I don't think it'll be a problem. She comes around once a month and Enrique slips her a bottle of his best scotch."

"Okay, hang on to the keys just in case. Enrique in his office?"

"Oh yeah, back booth, same old, same old."

It was only noon; however, there were already three tough looking men, bathed in tattoos, leaning on the bar drinking beer from bottles. "Hey guys," Brett said, as he headed to the back of the room. One man nodded his head, the others ignored him.

Manny eyed Brett coming in and slid further into the booth to make room.

Enrique stood up and shook his hand. "How you doin', Brett?"

Brett extended his hand. "I'm pretty worried actually."

They sat down in the booth. "Anything new?" Manny asked.

"I got a call from a homicide detective with the New York City Police. Someone was killed there, and they found a pill bottle that belonged to Annie."

"Did they say it was her?" Enrique asked, with trepidation.

"No, they wouldn't even confirm that someone was killed, but why else would the homicide division be calling. They asked if Annie was missing."

"What did you say?"

"I told them no, and I'd have her call them. They knew I was lying."

Enrique put his hand over Brett's. "We don't know who's dead. What reason would they have to kill Annie?"

"None, but desperate people do desperate things."

Manny raised his shot glass and signaled the bartender for another. "We need to get proof she's okay. When are you expecting a call?" Enrique asked.

"Probably tomorrow, but they always distort the voice."

"Ask to talk to her. Tell 'em you don't trust 'em."

The bartender put a shot glass filled with Tequila in front of Brett. "Drink it," Manny ordered.

Brett leaned his head back and threw the drink down his throat. He coughed and took a gulp out of Manny's water glass. "What if they won't let me?"

"Then we'll move on and assume she's all right."

Brett didn't look too encouraged. "Maybe I should bring the police in."

"Don't do that yet," Enrique said. "If, God forbid, Annie is gone, the police can't help, but if she's okay, we may have a better chance of getting her back than they do."

"What should I say when they call me?" Brett asked, feeling very nervous about the idea of deceiving the police.

"Avoid them. Filter all your calls through the answering machine and tell Ginger to say you're on vacation."

A knot was forming in Brett's stomach. "What about the money? I haven't tried to liquidate anything yet."

Enrique put his hand over Brett's again. "Here's the deal buddy. I can get you two million in hundred dollar bills, but most of it will be funny money."

"You mean counterfeit?" Brett asked.

"Most of it."

"What good is that?"

"Brett, these people are amateurs, the chance they can spot phony dough is slim to none."

Brett looked worried. "But what if they can?"

"We provide a little insurance so they won't," Enrique said.

"I don't get it."

"Okay, follow the math. If we put fifty $100 bills in a packet, each packet will then contain $5 thousand. We'll prepare four hundred packets which will equal $2 million."

"I get that, but what's the insurance you talked about?"

Enrique grinned. "The top bill on each packet will be a genuine $100 bill. If they check the top of any packet, it will test real."

"So we use four hundred genuine $100 bills. That's forty thousand dollars. Where do we get those?" Brett asked.

"You buy them," Enrique answered. "You pay the $40 thousand up front for the real money."

"What about the funny money? What's that cost?"

"You pay the supplier 10% up front, $200 thousand."

"So I put up a total of $240 thousand?"

"That's right, but here's the good part. If we can recover the money from the kidnappers, we can return it to our supplier."

"Then what?" Brett asked.

"Then you get your $40 thousand in genuine money back and you only pay half the fee for renting instead of buying the counterfeit money. Total cost, $100 thousand, even."

"What if they get away with all the money?"

"Then hopefully we get Annie back for only $240 thousand instead of $2 million."

"Do we have a plan to get the money back?" Brett asked.

Enrique took out a cigarette and lit it with his monogrammed lighter. He inhaled deeply and then exhaled. As he watched the cloud drift toward the ceiling, he said, "Go back to work and wait for their call. You'll get instructions from them, but don't worry; I'm guessing we're a lot smarter than they are."

Brett got up to leave and both Enrique and Manny jumped up to embrace him. "Liquidate the $240 thousand as soon as possible," Enrique said. "Remember, our goal is to get Annie back whatever it costs."

As he started for the door Manny asked, "You all right, buddy?"

Brett gave a weak smile. "I'm fine," he answered, as he nodded goodbye and retrieved his keys from Omar.

Chapter Eighteen

San Carlos, Ca.
September 3, 2001

Brett tried to sleep, but he kept tossing, his thoughts returning to Annie. Where was she? Was she safe? Would he see her again? Finally he closed his eyes and locked his roving brain onto the memory of the happiest day of his life.

Brett and Annie were in Palm Beach, Florida for five weeks. Brett rented a huge estate on the island as a headquarters from which they and a group of colleagues were executing a deceptive plan to recover $5.5 million of fraudulent insurance payouts from J.T. and his wife Maria.

It was February 4th, 2001, twenty-one years since Brett and Annie's first wedding. This day was much sweeter. Being divorced for five years had actually strengthened their relationship. Brett had never stopped loving Annie, but he knew he was responsible for their breakup and he was working hard not to repeat his mistakes. Annie had been through a tumultuous marriage to J.T., which had brought her to the realization that she was still in love with Brett.

It was an odd guest list, only six people: Enrique and his wife Marcella, Manny and his girlfriend Carmen, Enrique's bodyguard Omar, and Rob, a young Silicon Valley millionaire who owned his own private jet. By 10 p.m. the festivities had died down and everyone retired to their rooms. "Let's throw on some shorts and take a drive." Brett said.

"It's kind of late, don't you think?" Annie answered.

"I'm not really tired and it's seventy-five degrees outside. What about it?"

"Sure, why not."

Brett slipped on a pair of loose linen shorts and a Hawaiian shirt; Annie put on a pair of short shorts and a halter top. They jumped into the rented Escalade and Brett opened the sun roof and headed down South Ocean Boulevard, along the beach, toward the tip of the island. The moon was full and as they drove its beam appeared to be dancing along with them as it reflected off the water.

"How does it feel to be married again?" Brett asked.

"Feels good, you?"

Brett reached over and squeezed her hand. "Feels great. Ever dream five years ago this would happen?"

"Never, but I never dreamed our old friend and

my second husband, J.T., would turn out to be a crook either."

"Does that make me your third husband or your first husband once removed?"

Annie laughed out loud, she knew he was kidding, and said, "You're so full of it."

"Some things never change," Brett said.

Annie leaned over and kissed him on the cheek and said, "But I love you anyway."

Ahead Brett could see the lights of R. G. Kreusler Park, one of the few public beaches on the island. He pulled into the parking lot and drove to the far end which was dimly lit and had a good view of the ocean. He parked a hundred yards from the nearest car and they both sat in silence soaking in the view until Annie broke the spell. "Do you think this con job on J.T. and Maria is going to work?"

"It's going to work. Remember this is a 'Day job' for Enrique and Manny; they've been in the underworld all their lives."

"I don't care that they're small time gangsters, I like them, and Marcella and Carmen are really great women. Hell, even Enrique's bodyguard, Omar, as scary as he looks, is a sweet guy."

"I agree, and friendship and loyalty are more important than money to them."

"Tell me again how you met them."

"I treated Enrique's son when he got his mouth

banged up in an accident. When I needed help looking into that nasty stuff in Baja that J.T. was involved with, he loaned Manny to me. We've been friends ever since."

"Well, they're really fond of you."

"I feel the same toward them." They fell back into silence until Brett leaned over the center console dodging the gear shift lever, and gave Annie a kiss on the lips. "I love you," he whispered.

She tried to put her arms around his shoulders but it was too awkward. "Should we get in the back seat?" she asked.

"I thought you'd never ask," Brett joked, as he reclined his seatback.

Annie crawled onto the rear seat and flipped the mechanical lever that flattened the leather seats into a horizontal position. Brett made sure the doors were locked and shimmied back to join her.

Annie lay flat on her back and Brett nuzzled in beside her. "Something in your shorts pocket is poking me?" She said.

Brett laughed, "These shorts don't have pockets," he answered, as he put his arm around her and drew her close. "That halter is in my way, any chance it's removable?"

Annie reached behind her back and undid the clasp. "That better?" she said, as she let it drop to the floor.

Brett put his lips to hers and gently fondled her

exposed nipples. Since Annie had never given birth, her breasts were as firm as they were twenty years ago. He broke the kiss and moved his head down to her breasts and began gently sucking. Annie stroked the back of Brett's head and put her lips on his neck as she felt his saliva dripping down toward her navel.

Brett worked his way back to her lips and Annie opened her mouth and let his tongue caress hers. His right hand inched its way down to the three buttons on the front of her shorts and he undid them and slipped his hand inside and between her legs. He could feel the heat and the moisture on her hair as he slowly and softly slid a finger inside.

Annie arched her back, reached down and slithered out of her shorts, and then laid back on the leather as Brett caressed her. The excitement of her being stark naked while he was still fully clothed, and the feel of his erection against her leg, separated only by the smooth linen of his shorts, brought her to a quick and strong climax. She relaxed and lay still with her eyes closed.

Brett slipped out of his shorts and quickly unbuttoned his shirt. Now Annie could feel the heat from his body, and she pulled him close and began to rotate her hips around him. With each rotation he went deeper inside her until their bodies were locked together. Annie pushed up on one elbow and rolled them over; now she was looking down at Brett.

Slowly she began to grind her pelvis against him and then she lifted her hips up and let them drop back down. She kept the movement going while she increased the cadence. Brett couldn't hold back against her sensual movements and let himself release as he pulled her down on him as hard as he could.

They lay in the same position for five minutes before Annie rolled off, looked at the steamed up windows and said, "Reminds me of college days."

"I never remember it being that good in college." Brett said, as he sat up and glanced out the window. "Oh, oh, a patrol car just pulled into the other end of the lot."

They both started laughing hysterically as they scrambled for their clothes and haphazardly put them on. Quickly they jumped back onto the front seats and Brett started the car as he brought the seat backs to the upright positions. Just as the car approached, Brett flipped on his headlights and drove off. "Bet I know what those cops are saying."

"What?" Annie asked.

"Damn kids." Brett answered.

Brett popped his eyes open and looked at the ceiling of his bedroom where the moonlight was peeking around a cloud and filtering in through the skylight. He smiled for the first time in a week and drifted off to sleep.

CHAPTER NINETEEN

San Carlos, Ca.
September 4, 2001

He was going through the motions working on patients, but his heart wasn't in it. The note Brett picked up in Stovepipe Wells gave him seven days to come up with $2 million. Today was day seven, he knew the call was coming from the abductors, and he was ready for it.

At ten minutes after two, Ginger appeared in the treatment room doorway. "Dr. Raven, can you take a phone call?" she asked, already knowing the answer.

Brett excused himself from the room, slipped off his gloves and mask, and entered his private office. There it was again; the red button on the phone panel blinking ominously. He pushed it and spoke into the receiver, "Raven."

"Do you have the money?" The slurred and distorted voice asked.

"Most of it," he answered.

"What do you mean most of it?"

"It's a lot to come up with in seven days. I'll have it all by tomorrow."

There was silence on the line and then the voice said, "You realize your wife's life is dependent upon your coming up with that money."

"I understand, but I need to talk to her. I need to know she's safe."

"Trust me, she's safe.'

"Why should I trust a motherfucker like you?' Brett spewed.

"My what a filthy mouth you have doctor. If I didn't have a thick skin, I'd be insulted."

"Okay, cut the bullshit, I'll have the two million tomorrow, but I'm not about to turn it over without proof that Annie is alive and unharmed."

"You'll have the proof before you turn over the money. We'll call you tomorrow and give you instructions for the exchange of the money for your wife. Remember, all hundred dollar bills."

"I'm not doing it unless I talk to Annie right now."

"You're not getting this doctor. I know you don't like it, but we're in control here not you. You'll talk to her when we say it's time to talk to her. In the meantime you'll get that money. We all know that, so don't act tough and threaten us. By the way if we see any sign of police or FBI, you can kiss your babies goodbye also."

Brett began to speak, but his mouth went dry.

"Tomorrow," the voice repeated, and then the phone went dead.

Brett hung up the desk phone, picked up his cell and dialed the Redwood City number.

"Enrique," the voice answered.

"They called," Brett said.

"Did they give you more time?"

"Till tomorrow."

"What about Annie?"

Brett began to shiver and his voice quivered. "They said I'd be able to talk to her before I give them the money."

"You all right?" Enrique asked.

"I'm scared. I don't know if I'm doing the right thing here. I'm trying to block it out, but I keep thinking of that call from the New York homicide detectives. Someone is dead and I keep thinking it may be Annie."

Enrique spoke in a soft manner, much like a father counseling a son. "Brett, we have to assume she's okay, we agreed on that. I still think we can handle this better than the cops, but it's up to you. It's your call."

Brett was silent and Enrique knew he was processing all the information; he didn't say a word. Finally Brett said, "Enrique, you've always come through for me. If you think we should leave the police out of it, I trust your judgment. Where do I go from here?"

"Okay, first of all did you liquidate the two hundred

and forty thousand?"

"I've got it. I took it out of my retirement plan."

"Good, have a cashier's check made out to cash and drop it by my office this afternoon. I'll have the packets of $100 bills banded with a good bill on top of each wad. Call me tomorrow after you talk to those pricks. Remember our first goal is to exchange the money for Annie, our second is to get the money back since you'll have $240 thousand at stake."

Doubt began to creep in again. "How, how're we going to do that?" Brett asked.

"One step at a time: first Annie, then the money. Agree to all of their demands when they call. Don't worry, we can change them up later. Believe me, the next call won't be their last."

"Okay," Brett whispered.

"Brett."

"Yeah."

"I want you to have dinner with Manny tonight."

"Why?"

"He's riding shotgun on this."

"Enrique, I can…"

"No arguing, meet him at Il Fornaio in Palo Alto around seven."

"Okay, see him there."

Brett gave his car keys to the attendant and opened the door to the restaurant. He hadn't been here in years, but it was just as he remembered it, full Italian décor and the tantalizing aroma of garlic, tomatoes, and basil.

Manny was in the bar and spotted him walking in. He jumped off his stool and placed a hand on each of Brett's shoulders. "How you doin', buddy?"

Brett hugged him back and said, "I thought I was pretty tough, but this is brutal, not knowing if she's safe and not being able to do anything to help her."

Manny released his grip and said, "We're goin' to get her back. I'm with you on this."

They hoisted themselves onto bar stools just as a pretty brunette with a butch haircut pushed two cocktail napkins in front of them. "Two glasses of Sangiovese," Manny said, to the barkeep.

"I don't know what I'd do without you guys," Brett said.

"Brett, I've seen you operate down in Baja and back in Palm Beach. You are tough and we're goin' to kick ass as soon as the first round bell goes off. We just have to wait for it."

The red wine was set in front of them by the bartender's assistant. "Dinner?" she asked.

"I'm not real hungry," Brett responded.

"Two linguini and clams and sourdough with olive oil," Manny instructed. "Brett, I know you, you're an in-charge type of guy. This is getting to you because right now they're calling the shots. The game will change, believe me."

"You sure?"

"I'm sure.   Enrique said you're getting the instruction call tomorrow. That right?"

"Looks that way, I gave Enrique the check this afternoon."

"You won't believe how real the money's goin' to look. We've used these guys before. It would take a pro from the Treasury Department to tell it's fake."

"You know Manny, I don't give a shit if it costs me the whole two forty. I just want Annie back."

"Hey, man, I was at your wedding seven months ago; I know how much you love her. It's like Enrique said, first we get Annie, then we focus on getting the money back."

The pasta was set in front of them with steam rising from the deep bowls. Manny separated a piece of bread from the loaf, dipped it in the oil and then in the clam sauce. "Eat a little," he said. "You're goin' to need some energy for the next few days."

Brett took a forkful of pasta and twirled it into a ball against his pasta spoon. He tried to get it into his mouth but he just couldn't eat. He let it fall back into the bowl.

Chapter Twenty

New York City, N.Y.
September 5, 2001

His corduroy sport coat was getting old and showing signs of wear. After all, O'Hara had worn it to work every day for the last year. He took it off, wiped the doughnut crumbs from the lapel and hung it on the back of his chair. He spotted Czychowitz coming out of the coffee room. "Hey, Al, we have anything new on the Times Square murder?"

"Oh, hey there, Pat. Yeah, I ran a search on that gal Annie Raven from California. Pretty weird."

"How so?"

"Well, she marries this dentist, Brett Raven in 1980 and divorces him in 1995. Then she goes and marries a guy named John Thomas Talbot. Recognize that name?"

"The Times Square Hotel," Pat replied.

"Right, now here's where it gets really weird.

Last year she gets an annulment from Talbot even though he was reported dead in a plane crash, and then she marries Raven again."

O'Hara scratched his head. "Why do you think the husband lied to us about her being in New York?"

"Maybe he didn't know or maybe he knew and he's involved."

"You suggesting a love triangle."

"Could be, but then what was the private dick doing in the room?" Al asked, rhetorically.

"Maybe he was paid to bring the woman there." Pat replied.

"You think she was there against her will?"

"Maybe, but it still raises the question, why did the husband lie to us." Pat answered.

"Think he's the shooter?"

"Beats me, I ran a weapons check and there's nothing registered to him, but hell, over half the guns in this country aren't registered.

"So where are we?" Czychowitz asked.

O'Hara took a yellow legal tablet out of his drawer and started to scribble on it. "Okay, we've placed three people in the hotel room: The ex-husband Talbot, the ex-wife Annie, and the P.I. Erskine. One is dead from a pistol shot to the forehead and the other two are long gone. The dentist in California denies his wife is missing, even though we know she is."

"Where do we go from here?" Al asked.

"The dentist, Raven, obviously knows more than he's telling us. He's the key to the case. If we're going to solve it, we need a face-to-face with him."

"His place or ours?"

"You feel like a one day back and forth to California? United has a flight out to Frisco at six p.m. We can catch up with the tooth doc tomorrow and get a flight back in the afternoon."

"Book it," Al said.

"We've got a few hours," Pat said, glancing at his watch. "Find out all you can on the husband. I've got a hunch I want to follow up on. Meet you at the gate."

Czychowitz kept looking at his watch. The plane was already boarded and the jetway doors were getting ready to close when he spotted O'Hara running toward the gate. "Where you been? Another minute and we'd have missed it."

"Was waiting for a report. Come on we'll talk on the plane."

The detectives were able to get the last two seats on the flight; unfortunately Al was in row 67 and Pat in row 71. After the pilot had reached altitude and was safely in cruise, O'Hara got out of his seat and approached a young guy with long hair and no deodorant who was sitting next to Czychowitz. He had a Sony Walkman on his lap and a miniature headset over his ears and was tapping his finger on the armrest while keeping time with the music. "Mind changing seats with me?" O'Hara asked. "My buddy here and I need to talk."

"What?" The guy from GQ asked while taking off the headset.

"I'm traveling with your neighbor," Pat said. "How 'bout changing seats?"

"Screw you, man, I'm listening to music here."

"That's not very polite," Czychowitz said, leaning over and banging two knuckles against the guy's sternum.

"The fuck," the young guy shrieked, as he rubbed his chest and prepared for retaliation.

Czychowitz quickly took out his wallet and flipped it open revealing a gold New York Police badge. Pat did the same. "Okay, I don't want any trouble," the guy said, as he got out of his seat and started back to row 71. As he squeezed by O'Hara, he whispered in his ear. "Fuck you and your buddy."

Pat laughed and sat down next to Al. "Pretty tough guy," Al said.

"Yeah, real tough. So what did you find on the dentist?"

Al took out a little notebook and glanced

through it. "He's a pretty straight shooter. No record, not even a traffic ticket. Lived in the community for twenty years, has a good dental practice there. He's a private pilot and owns his own plane."

"Did ya check the FAA records?"

"I'm getting there," Czychowitz answered. "He had a partner in an airplane named John Thomas Talbot. Last year Talbot crashed the plane in Baja, Mexico and was supposedly burned up in it."

"So the guy that married his ex-wife was previously his partner."

"Exactly, but here's the best part, Raven took a flight a couple days ago, guess where?"

"I assume you're going to tell me," Pat said.

"Las Vegas, Nevada with a stop at airport L09, Stovepipe Wells, California."

"Son of bitch," Pat murmured.

"So what report almost made you miss the plane?"

"Oh yeah, almost forgot, I checked out our detective Elmer, who incidentally goes by the name Biff. He has a registered weapon."

"Let me guess," Al said. "A Beretta."

"You got it."

Chapter Twenty-One

San Carlos, Ca.
September 5, 2001

Brett arrived at his office a half hour before his eight o'clock patient. Ginger was already there getting charts in order for the twenty-three patients on his schedule. "Grab some coffee, I'll meet you in the back office," Brett said, as he picked up a copy of the upcoming day's schedule.

Ginger knocked and entered before Brett could acknowledge her. She handed him a cup and kept one for herself as she settled into the relaxer opposite Brett's desk. "Good news or bad?" she asked.

Brett took a gulp of coffee. "A little of both, some cops from New York City called me."

"New York? Is she in New York?"

Brett didn't mention the detectives were from the homicide division. "I think so; I'm guessing I'll be going there soon."

"How soon?"

"Soon!"

"Brett you have twenty three patients today not counting the emergencies that will drop in. The next seven or eight days look the same."

"I'm sorry, Ginger. You know I wouldn't go if I didn't have to. Can you load John up a little heavier? He's young and needs the income."

"I'll figure it out. Just find Annie and bring her home."

"Thanks, by the way you may get a call from those cops wanting to talk to me. I really want to avoid them for the time being, so feed them a little B.S. and tell them I'll get back to them."

"Okay, but I don't get it, are they on to the kidnappers?"

"I'm not sure what they're on to, but they told me they think Annie is back there."

Ginger was still confused and sensed Brett preferred it that way, so she dropped the subject. "Will you have your cell with you? I may have to get in touch."

"No problem, call me whenever."

They sat in silence just sipping the coffee. Ginger was smart and she was beginning to put a few pieces together. Finally she asked, "You getting another call this morning?"

"Yeah, you know the drill."

"When should I start thinning the schedule?"

"I can make it till noon, but after that it's iffy."

Ginger looked at her watch. "Okay, I'll start right now." She got up to leave. As she approached the door she stopped. "Brett?"

"Yeah."

"Are you in danger?"

"Don't know, but Manny will be with me just in case."

Ginger let out the breath she was holding. "I'm starting to like that guy," she said, as she left for the front desk.

It was 10:20 and Brett was working on his fifth patient of the morning when he spied Ginger in the hallway holding her fist to her ear. He excused himself and went to his private office. There it was again, the blinking red button of anxiety. He punched it. "Raven."

"Goood moorninng," the disguised voice droned.

"Fuck you," Brett responded.

"Do you have the money?" the slurred voice asked, ignoring the insult.

"Yeah, I have it."

"Is it in one hundred dollar bills?"

"Wrapped nice and tidy, now how do I get Annie back?"

"How's that little Baron of yours running?"

The voice asked, ignoring Brett's question.

"Why, you want that too?"

The voiced chuckled. "No, you can keep it, but you'll have to bring the money to New York City, and I don't think it's a good idea to bring it on an airliner. You know where Teterboro Airport is?"

"Never been there, but I can find it."

"Good, tomorrow is the 6th; we'll expect you on the 8th. There's a room waiting in Manhattan at the St. Regis on 5th and 55th. We figured since you're such a big spender you wouldn't mind the luxury. Your reservation is for only two nights, don't make us extend it!"

"What about A..." He heard a click and the line was dead.

Brett struggled through his morning patients, and then headed for Redwood City. Omar greeted him with a high fist clasp and a pat on the back. "He's in the booth," Omar said, pointing to the back of the bar.

Brett slid in next to Manny and facing Enrique. "You got the call?" Enrique asked.

"Yeah, they want me to fly the money in my plane to Teterboro in New Jersey."

"Then what?"

"Check into the St. Regis. I guess they'll contact me there."

"That's good. I was worried about you getting

on a United flight with $2 million in counterfeit money." He reached under the table and with both hands lifted a soft leather satchel onto the Formica counter top. It was only about twenty inches square, a lot smaller than Brett had imagined it would be. Enrique clicked open the locking clasp located on the top of the case and spread the sides apart, exposing the four hundred packets of fifty one hundred dollar bills piled neatly inside. "How's it look?" He asked.

Brett peered in. "Oh, my God, I've never seen that much money in my life."

Enrique smiled, "But how does it look?"

Brett took out one of the packages. None of the bills looked brand new, as if they had just been printed. They all appeared to be currency that had been in circulation for some period of time. "Real," he said. "How much does this case weigh?"

"Money weighs forty-four and half pounds and the case about four. No problem for a fit guy like you."

Brett returned the packet of bills to its place in the stack, folded the sides of the case together and snapped the clasp shut. "What now?' he asked.

"When d'ya plan on leaving?"

"I need to plan the flight and get the plane ready. Probably take off about five tomorrow morning."

Manny spoke for the first time. "I'll pack a few

things and meet you at four-thirty."

"That'll work," Brett said, and then turned back to Enrique. "What do we do when they contact me at the St. Regis?"

"Rely on Manny; he's been through this kind of shit before. Don't hesitate to give them the money if you can get Annie back safely, but don't take any crap from them either. Remember, they don't want to be stuck with her. All they want is to get their hands on the money. You have more control than you think."

Brett smiled for the first time. "It would almost be worth two hundred and forty thousand to imagine the looks on their faces when they find out the money's counterfeit."

Enrique and Manny joined in with a laugh. "Let's hope it doesn't come to that," Manny said. "I'll meet you at the San Carlos Airport at four thirty tomorrow morning."

"See you tomorrow," he said, to Manny. "Thanks, buddy," he said to Enrique as he headed toward the front door with the $2 million hoisted over his left shoulder.

Chapter Twenty-Two

San Carlos, Ca.
September 5, 2001

Usually either Brett or Annie phoned Samantha once a week to make sure everything was going well with the pregnancy. Brett had just seen the telephoto pictures that had been taken of Samantha. The kidnappers knew who she was and where she lived.

"Brett, is that you?" Samantha asked, after answering the phone.

"Yes, it's me. We haven't talked in a while.

"I was going to call Annie. She was supposed to pick me up for a lunch date last week, but she never made it. Is she okay?"

"Oh, sorry about that, she came down with the flu and she's been in bed for a week. I was supposed to call and apologize for her, but it slipped my mind, so here I am a week late."

"No problem, I was just concerned because it

wasn't like her to miss an appointment. Tell her to get well soon."

"I will. How you been feeling?" Brett asked.

"Great. It's a little hard to sleep and my ankles are pretty swollen, but I've been here before. Everything's pretty normal; I'm not concerned."

"That's good to hear. Think you'll make it all the way to the due date in October?"

"Who knows? It feels like the twins are ready to push out any minute, but I know the last six weeks always feel this way."

"I wouldn't know," Brett replied. "I can't even imagine how it must feel with a belly full of babies."

"Brett, it feels wonderful, really! I love it."

He wanted to fish for clues but didn't want to startle her. "Everything normal around the house?" he asked.

"What do you mean normal?"

"I don't know, just making sure you're safe 'n sound."

"Typical prospective father, always seeing danger lurking. I'm fine and the babies are safe and warm."

"Sorry, guess I'm a little paranoid. Hey, Annie and I will be away for a couple weeks."

"Where you going?"

"Just a little vacation before we have to start changing diapers, maybe Lake Tahoe."

"That's a good idea. You won't have any time for R & R after the babies arrive."

"We'll try to check in, but I didn't want you to worry if you didn't hear from us for a week or two."

"No problem, have fun."

"Thanks, we will."

"And Brett?"

"Yes?"

"Thanks again, for letting me be a part of this."

"You're so welcome. Talk to you in a week or two."

"See ya," Samantha said.

Brett hung up the receiver and stared at the phone for at least thirty seconds. "Stay strong," he whispered to himself.

CHAPTER TWENTY-THREE

San Carlos, Ca.
September 6, 2001

"May I help you?" Ginger said to the man in the corduroy jacket.

"Yes, ma'am." He replied, as he opened his wallet exposing a gold badge. "I'm Detective O'Hara and this is Detective Czychowitz. We're with the New York City Police Department. Could we speak with Dr. Raven?"

"You could if he were here, but he isn't."

"Will he be here soon?" Czychowitz asked, with an edge to his tone.

"I'm afraid not," Ginger replied. "He left on vacation early this morning."

Al gave Pat an incredulous look. "I find that hard to believe. We just talked to him a few days ago and he didn't mention anything about a vacation."

"I'm sorry, but does Dr. Raven usually supply you with his daily itinerary?"

The smirk on Czychowitz's face disappeared and was replaced with a grimace. "Ma'am, we're investigating a homicide here, we don't need any smart-aleck remarks from you."

"My name's not ma'am, it's Ginger, and I'm not crazy about your attitude either."

Pat stepped in. "Ginger, we're sorry if we got off to a bad start, but this is serious and we need answers to some questions. Did you know Dr. Raven's wife was in New York?"

"I'm just a receptionist; doctor and Mrs. Raven don't share their personal lives with me."

"You must know that Mrs. Raven is missing." Al said.

"I told you, I just answer the phones and make appointments. I had no idea Annie was missing."

"Do you always call Mrs. Raven by her first name?" Pat asked. "You said you weren't on a personal basis with the Ravens."

"I'd like to see those badges again." Ginger said.

Ignoring the request, Czychowitz asked, "Ever heard of a guy named J.T. Talbot?"

"Never," Ginger lied.

"How 'bout Biff Erskine, that name ring a bell?" Pat asked.

"Did you say Buff Foreskin? Spell that, will you?"

"You heard it right the first time, Ginger. Do you recognize it or not?" Pat said, in an uncharacteristically angry manner.

"I asked again to see your badges; are you going to show them to me or not?" Ginger answered.

Pat nodded at Al and both detectives opened their wallets and exposed their gold shields. "Ma'am… uh Ginger, are you satisfied?" O'Hara asked.

"Did you guys ever see the movie Beverly Hills Cop?" Ginger asked.

Both men looked at each other blankly and then Al said, "I guess so, but what has that got to do with anything?"

"Remember, Axel Foley, the detective from Detroit who went out to Beverly Hills chasing bad guys?"

"Yeah, so," Al said.

"So he got into big trouble because he didn't have jurisdiction in California and he didn't check in with the Beverly Hills Police Department. Have you checked in with the San Carlos Police Department?"

Pat looked a little sheepish. "Well, actually… actually we just got here and haven't had a chance but…"

Ginger interrupted. "I'll be here till five. Feel free to stop back after you do that," she said, as she closed the sliding glass partition to the waiting room.

The detectives retreated to their rented Ford Escort. "We really goin' to check in with the locals?" Al asked Pat.

"Waste two hours with some hick desk cop, no fuckin' way. Even though she has some answers, she isn't going to give us any of them anyway. Let's look somewhere else."

"What are you thinking?"

"I've got a hunch she was telling the truth when she said Raven left town. Let's head down to the local airport where he keeps that plane he flew to Stovepipe Wells."

Pat parked the car in the lot facing the terminal that housed a lobby, an administration office, an aviation store, and a small diner called the Sky Kitchen Café. "Might as well eat breakfast," Pat said.

In the center of the café was an island counter with twelve swivel stools. They took seats between a couple guys, who they quickly recognized from their conversation, were local pilots. After ordering the egg scramble special along with a cup of coffee, Al turned to one of the locals, a guy with a leather jacket and a weather beaten face. "Come here often?"

"Every day," he replied, while wedging a

toothpick between his upper front teeth. "Your first time here?"

"Yeah, we're from down south, driving up to Sacramento and thought we might run into an old buddy who flies out of here."

"Really, who?"

"Brett Raven, my brother went to dental school with him." Al said, as he sampled the egg dish that had been set in front of him.

"I know Brett well. Always call him the Jaw Breaker just to piss him off."

"Seen him around today?" Pat asked, as he leaned around to get into the conversation.

The local turned to the other six men sitting at the counter. "Hey, any of you guys seen Raven this morning?"

A well dressed, middle aged man who looked more like a banker than a pilot said, "I saw him late yesterday at his hangar. Looked like he was pre-flighting his Baron for a trip."

"Maybe we'll look in his hangar, see if he's still there. Which one is it?" Pat asked.

"First row to the south, Charlie five."

Pat picked up the check. "I got it," he whispered to Al. We'll bill it to the department."

Al shrugged. "Sounds good to me. Let's make a stop at the administration office."

"Just what I was thinking," Pat responded.

Two women were working in the office, but only one looked up when the detectives walked in. "Help ya?" she asked.

Pat took out his wallet and displayed his badge. This time without mentioning New York, he said, "Police, any chance you have a key to hangar Charlie five?"

"I'm sure we do, is something wrong?"

"Just checking for a reported stolen airplane," Al said.

The woman laughed. "I don't think Brett Raven is the type to steal an airplane."

Al smiled back. "It may have been hot when he bought it. Could we have that key?"

The woman scurried to a cabinet and retrieved a key labeled C-5 and handed it to Pat. "Make sure you bring it back," she said.

"Thank you ma'am, we'll only be a few minutes. By the way, what's the tail number of Dr. Raven's plane?"

"Six, Seven, Five, Nine Mike," she said, as she jotted it on a piece of scratch paper and handed it to Pat.

Pat opened the padlock and the two of them slid the heavy metal door along a track. The hangar was empty. "Looks like your hunch was right," Al said.

"Look through the papers on the desk, I'll check

the shop bench," Pat replied.

The desk was a hodgepodge of papers, sticky notes and airplane parts. Al pushed some radio knobs to the side and began examining the scraps of papers. After five minutes, Pat was back. "Nothin' on the work bench, you having any luck?'

"Couple phone numbers on stickies. This one looks like New Jersey." He handed the note to Pat.

Pat put his phone on speaker and dialed the number, 201-288-1775. "Teterboro Airport," a voice crackled across the speaker.

Pat put his thumb in the air to signal Al. "Is this the airport just across the river from Manhattan?" he asked.

"Yes, sir, right in the heart of the Meadowlands. What can I do for you?"

"Just checking my geography, thanks."

"No problem," the voice said, and hung up.

"You thinking what I'm thinking?" Al asked.

"Yeah, let's visit the control tower."

Pat pushed what looked like a house doorbell and a voice came through a speaker located next to it. "San Carlos Tower, can I help you?"

"Police, can we come up?"

A loud buzz came from the door as it popped ajar. The two detectives opened it and headed up the stairs to the observation platform where they were greeted by two men. "I'm Hank, this is Ted, what's up?"

The detectives exposed their badges and shook hands with Hank. Ted stayed busy with a set of binoculars giving instructions through a mic attached to a single ear headset. "Got five minutes?" Al asked.

"Sure," Hank said, "It's not very busy, Ted can handle it."

Al took the piece of scratch paper with Brett's tail number on it from his pocket and handed it to the controller. "Do you have a record of this plane taking off this morning?"

Hank changed pages on his computer screen and ran his finger down a list which had appeared on the new page. "Don't see it, what time do you think it left?"

"Maybe early," Pat said.

"That may be the problem. We don't open the tower till 7 a.m. Before that planes can take off without telling anyone."

"Can they fly out of the Bay Area without announcing their position or destination?"

"If they monitor the airspace and stay at the proper altitudes, sure"

"What about flight plans? I thought pilots have to file them," Al said.

Ted displayed a condescending grin. "Actually they don't, unless they're flying on an instrument flight. Most visual flights these days use a system called 'VFR Flight Following,' where the control centers follow them on radar. It's easier and safer."

"So if Five, Nine, Mike snuck out before your tower opened, who would they call if they wanted Flight Following?" Al asked.

"Probably NorCal Approach, they handle traffic below ten thousand feet within fifty miles of the Bay Area."

"What happens after fifty miles?"

"They get switched to Oakland Center who controls airspace from Hawaii to Nevada."

Pat took out his notepad and a pen. "Where would we go to talk to NorCal Approach or Oakland Center?"

Hank handed Pat a paper backed directory he had sitting on his desk. "You can keep this; I've got a dozen copies. The addresses and phone numbers are in there. Oakland is just across the bay in Fremont, but NorCal is up near Sacramento at Mather, the old Air Force field."

Pat took the pamphlet and stuffed it into his jacket pocket. "Thanks, Hank, appreciate it."

After returning the hangar keys the detectives sat in the rental car looking through the directory. "Let's give NorCal a call," Pat said, as he dialed a 916 area code.

"NorCal Tracon," the voice said.

"Pat O'Hara, NYPD, I need some information about a flight you may have handled this morning."

"Can you come into the office? I can't give out that info without seeing your credentials."

"We're up in the San Francisco Bay Area, can't spare the time."

"Sorry, sir, I just can't do it. Why don't you head over to Fremont? Oakland Center might be able to help."

Pat knew it was useless to argue about it. "Thanks, we'll try Oakland."

O'Hara crossed the Dumbarton Bridge and drove the thirteen miles from San Carlos to Fremont. Oakland Center was located in a one story gray stucco building with an over-sized parking lot and a sign FAA in front. Both men showed their badges and Pat asked to talk to the crew manager.

A bald headed man in his early fifties, wearing coke bottle glasses and drinking Pepsi from a can, came out of his office to greet them. "I'm Izzy, the day shift manager, what can I do for you?"

"We need to know if a twin engine Beech Baron requested Flight Following this morning," Al asked Izzy.

The manager logged their badge numbers into a loose leaf binder and then lit up the screen of his computer. "Give me the N number," he said.

Al read Brett's tail number off the now wrinkled piece of paper. "Six, Seven, Five, Nine, Mike."

The controller typed them into his data base. "Here it is, they checked in at 5:45 a.m. just west of Sacramento at thirteen thousand five hundred feet. Requested Flight Following to Rock Springs, Wyoming."

Al looked over the manager's shoulder pretending to understand the screen. That was almost five hours ago, any idea where they are now?"

"They were turned over to Salt Lake Center at 7:05 and Salt Lake turned 'em over to the Rock Springs, Wyoming, common traffic advisory frequency at 10:07 Mountain Time. Looks like they were there for about an hour. At 11:02 they were in the air again and requested Following to Des Moines, Iowa. My guess they'll be there around four o'clock Central time."

"Any idea where their next stop after Des Moines will be?" Pat asked.

"Won't know that till they request Flight Following again."

The detectives thanked Izzy and retreated back into their car. Pat got into the driver's seat and snuck a cigarette out of his pocket and lit it up. "Doesn't take a rocket scientist to see they're headed east. I'm guessing they'll stay in Des Moines overnight.

If we get back to New York by tomorrow morning, we can beat them to Teterboro."

"Okay, let's head back to the United Terminal," Al said. "Hey, I thought you quit."

"Don't tell my wife," Pat said, as he merged into traffic and headed back toward the bridge. "I'll owe her two hundred bucks."

CHAPTER TWENTY-FOUR

San Francisco, Ca. Airport
September 6, 2001

"Would you care for a glass of Champagne or something else to drink before we take off?" the flight attendant asked.

"Scotch for me," O'Hara said.

"Beer if you have it," Czychowitz replied. Turning to Pat he asked, "How the hell did you get us in first class?"

"It's called flashing the badge when all the coach seats are taken. Turns out the ticket agent's daddy is a retired cop."

"I knew there's a reason I chose you as my partner."

"You didn't choose me, I chose you," Pat said.

"Whatever, either way the seats are wide and the booze is free."

By the time the 737 was in cruise, both detectives had finished their first and were on their second drinks. "So what do we have?" Al asked, while stuffing a handful of cashews in his mouth.

"I've been thinking," Pat said. "Ginger knows Annie is missing, she knows who Talbot and Erskine are, and she knows Raven is on his way to New York. Why would she lie for him if she thought he was involved in a murder? She couldn't like the guy that much."

"Because, he's not involved?" Al asked.

"Exactly, Raven's wife is missing we know that. She was in a hotel suite in New York where a murder took place and now she's disappeared. One of the guys in that room is this J.T. guy who was supposedly dead, and by the way, used to be married to Raven's wife. This Biff character, who's also in the suite, is a hungry private dick. Why would Raven be racing to New York?"

"Not to have drinks with his wife's ex-husband and his bodyguard," Al answered.

"Yet, he's headed back there in a private plane instead of an airliner. I think we can forget the love triangle or even Raven as the shooter. This looks like a classic case of kidnap with murder thrown in as a bonus. Our prime suspect Raven is actually delivering the ransom."

"No question," Al replied. "Raven is trying to handle it on his own without bringing in law enforcement. That's why we can't make contact with him. Why do you think he's doin' that?"

Pat reflected. "Not sure, but we'll figure it out."

"Maybe if he'd brought us into it, there wouldn't be a dead body in the morgue."

"I doubt it. I think this case had a dead man walking before it started."

"You're probably right," Al agreed. "Think he has the money with him?"

"Raven? Why else would he make a grueling two day, fifteen hour flight in his own plane? He's afraid the money would be discovered on a commercial flight. Be hard to explain what a lot of cash is doing in your suitcase."

"How much do you think he's moving?"

"Your guess is as good as mine; a couple hundred thousand, maybe a million, maybe more."

"So if we get to him before he delivers the money and we confiscate it, he'll have no choice other than to play ball with us."

Pat smiled, "Now we're thinking alike. We should be at Teterboro well before he arrives, but let's keep a low profile and see where he goes and what he does with the money. We may get lucky, if not, we can pick him up whenever we want."

"What if he catches on and gives us the slip?"

Pat laughed, "This guy is out of his league, he'll be by himself in a strange city. What's the odds an egghead dentist from California will outsmart a couple New York cops in their own backyard. We'll get him by the balls, and if he doesn't cooperate, we'll squeeze."

Al ordered another beer to go with the filet that had been served on a fancy plate alongside a white linen napkin. "I can't wait to meet this jerk and see the look on his face when we take his money into custody. Without the cash he'll beg us to get to his wife's kidnappers and we'll have our killers."

"Get some sleep," Pat said. "We may have a long day tomorrow."

Chapter Twenty-Five

Des Moines, Iowa
September 7, 2001

6:00 a.m.

It was raining lightly when Brett and Manny got out of bed at the Airporter Motel. While Manny was in the shower Brett called the FAA for a weather briefing. "Baron Six, Seven, Five, Nine, Mike, we're in Des Moines and headed for Akron in about an hour. How's the weather look on our route?"

"Are you instrument capable?" the briefer asked.

Not the answer Brett was eager to hear; it usually meant bad weather ahead. "Yes," he replied. "Both the plane and the pilot are current."

"That's good, because we have a freaky low pressure system for this time of year in the area dropping rain and lowering visibilities on your route extending to about fifty miles west of Chicago. After that it looks pretty good with

152

scattered clouds and good visibility to the east."

"Any thunderstorms?" Brett asked.

"The three hour area forecast says slight chance of imbedded cells."

Brett listened to the rest of the briefing and filed an instrument flight plan from Des Moines to Akron, at 11,000 ft. He estimated the time en route as three hours and six minutes. "Okay, you're all set. Have a good flight and let Flight Service know if you encounter any unexpected weather," the briefer said.

"Will do, thanks," Brett replied, as he shut the cover on his cell phone.

Brett advanced the throttles and the twin 285 hp engines roared to life as the Baron sprinted down the runway. He pitched the nose up, entered the cloudy overcast at twelve hundred feet, and set the autopilot for a thousand foot per minute climb as he retarded the throttles and synched his props at 2500 rpm's. It was raining moderately at 11,000 ft. when he pushed the 'altitude hold' switch and reduced the power settings for cruise flight. The winds were blowing strongly from west to east at 31 knots adding 35 mph to the Baron's ground speed. Instead of its normal 208 mph, the instruments were indicating a blazing 243.

The first thirty minutes of the flight were bumpy, not concerning Brett, but just as the distance measuring equipment read a hundred east of Des Moines, the gray mist surrounding the Baron turned black, and the rain, now heavy, turned to hail. The noise from the pellets became so loud Brett turned the volume up on both radios and still he could barely hear them. The turbulence began to punish the plane, rocking it violently, and the autopilot was fighting valiantly to hold onto its altitude. Brett knew he had entered a thunderstorm cell. "You okay?" he asked Manny.

"Yeah, looks like we're in store for a Disneyland E-ride."

"Just pull your belts as tight as you can, we'll be all right."

Knowing the strong up and downdrafts were stressing the airplane's structure with the autopilot fighting against them, Brett disconnected it and took over manual control. He keyed his mic, "Minneapolis Center, Baron Five, Nine, Mike."

"Five, nine, Mike, Minneapolis center, go ahead."

"We're getting beat up pretty bad here at eleven thousand. What does your radar show?"

"Stand by," The controller said, as he changed computer screens. "Wow! No wonder you're getting whacked around, you're on the southern edge of a small line of thunder cells. Looks like fifty south will get you out of their way. You have permission to deviate at your discretion. I'd suggest a one six zero heading."

"Thanks," Brett said. "I'm not going to be able to hold an altitude. I'm getting big up and down drafts."

"No problem as long as you stay above three thousand. I'll call out any traffic."

"Roger that, Five, Nine, Mike, turning to a heading of one six zero."

The noise from the hail became deafening as it beat against the thin metal skin of the airplane and a bolt of lightning flashed and lit up the cockpit. "Don't look out," Brett told Manny, while he turned up all the lights in the cockpit to buffer the bright strikes. "The flashes will temporarily blind you."

"R…Roger that," Manny replied, with his voice shaking not from fear, but from the bumps that were straining his body against his seat and shoulder belts.

Within ten minutes the hail turned back to rain, the noise and buffeting began to dissipate, and the Baron became stable. Brett re-engaged the autopilot to hold seven thousand feet, the altitude to which the plane had on its own chosen to descend. He leaned back and took what seemed like his first breath of the last fifteen minutes. "How's the seat of your pants?" He asked Manny.

"I think it's sucked halfway up my rear end along with the seat cushion," Manny answered, as he loosened up on his seatbelt. "You done this before?"

"Once."

"Was it this bad?"

"I don't know, I crashed and got killed."

"That's not very funny. Anyway, good job, I owe you one."

The radio came alive. "Five, Nine, Mike, this is Minneapolis Center. How's the ride?"

"Getting smoother. Is the radar showing it clear enough to get back on course?" Brett asked.

"Yeah, looks good ahead. You may be interested, a 737 was in the cells at thirty-one thousand. He's got a lot of unhappy passengers. You're cleared back on course at seven thousand."

"Cleared back on course, thanks for your help, Five, Nine, Mike."

"No problem," the controller answered, as he clicked twice on his mic switch.

Two hours later in gorgeous sunshine, Brett squeaked the wheels onto runway seven at Akron International.

Weather wouldn't be a problem on the final

leg; however, the tricky airspace around New York City could be. Brett filed an instrument flight plan to ensure that controllers would vector him to Teterboro without violating any restricted airspace.

The distance from Akron to Teterboro was less than four hundred miles; with the strong tailwinds, Brett calculated they would only be in the air for an hour and forty-five minutes. It ended up almost two after New York Approach Control diverted them around traffic going in and out of Kennedy and La Guardia.

Brett taxied up to Signature Aviation and cut the engines. "I'll get the overnight cases, you grab the one with the money," he said to Manny.

Both men exited from the single door on the right side of the aircraft. Brett slid out last. "Oh, my God," he said, looking at the outside of the Baron.

"What?" Manny asked.

"Take a peek at the plane. All the paint is gone from the leading edges of the wings and there are dimples over the entire skin."

Manny looked along the wing. "Wow, that sucks. Covered by insurance?"

"Should be, but I've got bigger things to worry about. Let's go get Annie back."

Once inside the terminal, Brett took a place in

the line for rental cars while Manny stood guard over the cases. Teterboro is the closest airport to New York City for private planes to land and the lobby was packed with people. So packed, it was impossible for Brett or Manny to spot the guy in the corduroy jacket and his partner who was nonchalantly reading the New York Times.

CHAPTER TWENTY-SIX

Teterboro, New Jersey
September 7, 2001

2:05 p.m.

Brett threw the overnight cases onto the back seat; Manny kept the leather satchel with the treasure next to him in the front seat. Brett heard a beep coming from his cell phone and flipped open the cover to retrieve the message. "Hi, Brett, it's Ginger. Tried to get a hold of you yesterday, but you must have been in the air. I had two visitors from New York City, a detective named O'Hara and his a-hole partner Psycho Wits or something like that. Tried to pull the good cop, bad cop on me and I threw 'em out. Told 'em you were on vacation, but they didn't buy it. Better keep an eye open. Be safe and get Annie back."

Manny was watching Brett's expression and detected concern. "What's up?" he asked.

Brett handed him the phone, "Give a listen."

Manny listened to the message and flipped the cover shut. "You're not surprised are you?"

"Not really."

"Either am I, so let's just stay the course. Hand me that map."

Brett pushed the folded three page pamphlet toward Manny. "Looks like we can take the George Washington Bridge or the Lincoln Tunnel, any choice?" Manny asked.

"We're headed to midtown near Central Park. I think the St. Regis is on E. 55th near 5th Ave. Can you figure it out?"

Manny studied the map. "Looks like a push. Take I-95 south and we'll go through the tunnel."

As Brett merged from the frontage road onto the interstate, he caught Manny looking into the side view mirror. "Problem?" he asked.

"Not sure, there's a black Ford sedan a few cars back. It has the smell of cops."

"What do you want me to do?"

"Just drive normally, I'll keep an eye out."

It took about ten minutes before the signs for the Lincoln Tunnel came into view. Manny checked his mirror again. "Pull into the right lane and drop down to about twenty-five." he said.

Brett did as he was told and glanced into his rear view mirror. The black Ford, still five cars behind, also moved to the right. "Any ideas?" Brett asked.

Manny unfolded the map again and started running his fingers up and down the numbers and letters located on the side and top until they stopped at J-12. "When we come out of the tunnel head east on 40th, then turn north on Park and keep an eye open for Grand Central Station."

Brett had been in tight spots before with Manny and knew better than to start asking questions; he did what he was told. "When we get there, pull up in front, let me out, and come back for me in thirty minutes," Manny instructed.

The station was easy to spot; Brett had seen pictures of it in magazines dozens of times. He looked again into his mirror and saw that the Ford had missed the light on 42nd. He sped up and screeched to a halt in a loading zone in front of the station. Manny grabbed the leather satchel and burst out the passenger door. "Go," he said, as he ran full speed for the entrance to the train terminal.

Just as Brett popped the accelerator, the Ford made the turn into the Grand Central loading area. Spotting Brett pulling away, it didn't stop, but slowed down keeping a two car distance between them. Brett looked at his watch, 3:10. He took a right at 6th Ave. and drove all the way up to Central Park, then looped back and came down Lexington until he spotted Grand Central again on 42nd. He was right on time, 3:42. Manny seemed to appear from nowhere and jumped into the right seat as soon as Brett pulled to a halt. The leather satchel wasn't with him.

The black Ford was relentless and stayed on their tail for the twelve blocks to the hotel. Manny took a key out of his pocket, a stubby silver one with a round end and a red plastic handle with the yellow numbers 876 stamped on it. "Put this somewhere, but don't lose it" he said, as he handed it to Brett. Brett stuffed it into his front pants pocket.

"Welcome to the St. Regis," a doorman said, as he opened the driver's door for Brett. "Luggage?"

"We're good," Brett answered. "Just a couple of overnight cases."

The lobby was small, but oozed with old New York charm. Dark Oak trimmed the flocked wallpaper and high backed chairs, some with glass coffee tables nearby, were tastefully arranged throughout the room. Area carpets, either Turkish or Persian, were casually spaced over the hardwood floors and down the adjoining hallways. Brett approached the reception desk. "Doctor Raven, I believe I have a reservation."

The clerk looked intently at his computer screen. "Ah, yes, Dr. Raven," he said, as he looked up. "I see there are two of you, how about a couple kings?"

"Fine," Brett responded, and handed him his American Express.

The clerk completed the paperwork, handed two plastic key cards to Brett along with an envelope. "This was left for you," the clerk said.

As Brett and Manny were getting into the elevator, they both caught sight of two guys, one in a corduroy jacket, approaching the front desk.

They dropped their cases on the beds and Brett opened the envelope; the gold heart belonging to Annie's necklace fell into his hand. He slipped out a handwritten piece of paper. *We have your cell number. Expect a call at 6 p.m.*

A heavy knock came from the door. Brett handed the note to Manny. "Get rid of this," he said. Manny tore the note into small pieces and flushed it down the toilet as Brett went for the door.

Two men, both holding their wallets up exposing gold badges, greeted him. "New York Homicide, I'm detective Pat O'Hara, this is detective Al Czychowitz. Can we come in?"

"I guess you will whether I say yes or no."

The detectives closed the door behind them. "We talked to you a few days ago and you told us you would have your wife call us," O'Hara said.

"Guess I forgot," Brett answered.

"Pretty shitty memory for a doctor. You want

to tell us what's going on and why you flew all the way to New York in your own plane?" Czychowitz asked.

"Why don't you tell us why you're following us, then maybe we can exchange some information, Manny said.

Czychowitz looked at him with disdain. "Who the fuck are you anyway?"

"He's my associate," Brett said, sensing Manny's fuse getting short.

"Looks like a small time wise guy to me," Al answered.

Manny took a step toward Czychowitz, but Brett pushed him back. "Are you going to arrest us for flying to New York in a private plane?" Brett asked O'Hara.

"We told you on the phone a couple days ago that someone was shot to death in a hotel room, and we know your wife was in that room. Aren't you just a little concerned she might be the victim?" Pat asked.

"Was she?" Manny asked.

"Oh, the big shot is talking for you?' Czychowitz said to Brett.

"Was she?" Brett asked.

"Let's get some more information before we answer that question. What was she doing in a hotel room three thousand miles from home with her ex-husband and a private detective?"

"I don't know," Brett answered.

"Bullshit, you don't know. You know!" Czychowitz said, his voice raised and his steely gray eyes staring straight into Brett's. "Now tell us and maybe we can actually help you do whatever you're here to do." Brett didn't say a word.

"Gentlemen, don't bother to unpack, you're not spending tonight at the St. Regis. You're both under arrest as accomplices to murder." O'Hara said, as he removed two sets of cuffs from his belt.

"Come on, guys, you know we're not involved in a homicide," Brett said.

"Both of you place your hands behind your back. I'm sure your friend here knows the drill," Al said.

Pat snapped the cuffs on Brett and Manny and Al picked up the overnight cases. "Where's the third case you unloaded from your plane?" he asked.

"What third case?" Brett replied.

"You think we're stupid? I may not have graduated from dental school, but when it comes to murder, I'm a lot smarter than you." Al said. "I'll ask you again, where is that leather satchel?"

Brett and Manny were silent. "Okay, gentlemen, let's get you a new room. No king beds, I'm afraid." Pat said, as he nudged them toward the door.

The sliding metal gate slammed shut. Brett

had only heard that sound once before, when he had been thrown in a jail in Baja. He and Manny sat down on the metal bench which was supported to the wall by chains on each side. "Hey, guys," a squeaky voice said. Both Brett and Manny looked up. "Cam Clemente," the man said, thrusting out his hand from a bench across the cell.

Cam was a little guy, no taller than five foot five, with tan skin and non-descript features. Brett introduced himself and Manny and asked, "I know Clemente is a Puerto Rican name but I don't think Cam is. Where did that come from?"

The little guy started laughing hysterically exposing a set of once white, but now tobacco-stained, crooked, front teeth. "My real name is Angel, but my buddies call me Cam, like chameleon, because I can blend in anywhere without being seen."

"Yeah, if you blend so well, what got you in here?" Manny asked.

"Bogus arrest, bogus. Liquor store clerk said I lifted a pint of Jim Beam."

"Did you?"

"Yeah, but they can't prove it, I drank it while they were chasing me. When I got caught there was no evidence." He started laughing again."You guys are a little over dressed for this place. Why you here?"

Manny was sizing the little guy up. "Long story, Cam, any chance you could use a little cash?"

"Always," he answered. "Got a job for me?"

"Maybe," Manny said, as he heard keys jingling outside the cell.

"How do you like the accommodations?" Al asked, unlocking the cell door and stepping inside.

"Lovely, especially the private bath," Brett said, pointing to the stainless steel, seat-less toilet.

Czychowitz gave him a smug smile. "I wouldn't get too close to your roommate Cam over there. If he breaths on you, you'll probably get alcohol poisoning. By the way, Cam, the owner says if you'll give him eighteen bucks for the Beam, he'll drop the charges."

"If I had eighteen bucks I would have bought the bottle." Cam said.

"Maybe one of these guys will lend it to you; they're big spenders."

Manny shot Czychowitz a dirty look. "No problem, we'll cover it when you give us our wallets back."

"Speaking of personal effects," Al said, looking at Brett. "Mind telling me what the locker key we found in your pocket is for?"

"What key?" Brett asked.

"This one," Al said, dangling the yellow 876 in front of Brett.

He looked blankly at it. "No idea."

"Kind of a coincidence you dropped smart ass off at Grand Central and later we find a locker key in your pocket. We're headed over there right now and maybe we'll get lucky and bring your leather case back with us. By the way dinner will be here soon; you'll love it. Has mystery meat in it," Al said, as he walked out and signaled for a uniform to lock the cell door behind him.

When the detective was out of sight, Manny turned to Cam. "We'll cover you for the eighteen bucks. Give us a call at the St. Regis tomorrow morning before eight. I think you can make some money. Ask for Brett Raven's room."

Cam grinned, allowing two of his malposed teeth to pop out from under his upper lip, "Great, that's great. I can use some dough."

"What makes you think we're getting out of here tonight?" Brett asked Manny.

"Just a hunch," Manny answered. "Just a hunch."

Chapter Twenty-Seven

8:25 p.m.

"You goin' to eat any of that?" Cam asked.

"It's all yours," Manny replied, pushing the tray across the cement floor.

"Thanks, thanks," Cam said. "I always get hungry when the booze wears off."

Brett looked to his wrist for the time and remembered his watch had been confiscated along with his wallet, phone, shoes and belt. "What time do you think it is?" he asked Manny.

"Wall clock out there," he answered, "over the guard's desk."

Brett peeked out through the bars. "Damn it's eight-thirty; we missed the six o'clock call."

"Don't sweat it, with two million at stake, they'll call again," Manny said.

Cam's eyes got wide. "Two million, two million

dollars? I knew you guys were players. Wow, two million."

"Manny looked at Cam and said, "Buddy, this is mob money. You give us a hand and you make a grand, you screw up and a pint of liquor will be the least of your problems."

"Yes, sir, Manny sir, I get it. You can count on me."

"Remember, eight o'clock tomorrow morning."

"Got it. St. Regis, Brett Raven."

The hall door opened and O'Hara and Czychowitz walked in and signaled the night guard to open the cell. "Let's go guys, we have to talk."

The three cellmates got up off the benches. "Not you, numb nuts," Al said to Cam. "Just them."

Brett and Manny took seats on one side of a long coffee stained table, the detectives on the other side. Czychowitz looked at Manny. "Okay smart guy, what did you do with that leather satchel?"

"I put it in locker 876 at the train station," Manny replied.

"Then why was the locker empty?" O'Hara said.

Manny shrugged. "How would I know? I've been here in jail all evening."

The detectives looked frustrated, Brett looked perplexed, no one spoke. Finally O'Hara said to Brett, "We listened to your message from Ginger. She said 'be safe and bring Annie back.' What did that mean?"

"What do you think it meant?"

"We think your wife Annie was kidnapped by Talbot and Erskine. We think you brought the ransom money in that leather satchel, and we think you're trying to work around the police."

"Is that illegal?" Brett asked.

"No, but we still have a murder. The victim wasn't your wife, but she may be the killer. If you want to pay a ransom that's your business, but we're going to get our killer and if it's your wife, we'll arrest her after you get her back," O'Hara said.

"She's no killer," Brett replied.

"Then work with us and we'll get her back, and we'll get the real killer."

"Have to think about it," Brett said.

"Don't think too long, Czychowitz said. "I have a feeling your window is getting narrower. By the way, I answered a phone call on your cell at six o'clock, but the caller hung up. Was that the ransom call?"

"How should I know, you're the one who answered." Brett replied.

The detectives tone softened. "Look guys, we can help. Collect your stuff and you're free to go, but call us tomorrow. Here's my card," Pat said, as he handed it to Brett. "And Manny, no hard feelings, right?"

Manny forced a smile. "No, I love you guys."

As they were collecting their personal items, Brett said to Pat, "I want to cover Cam, how much to get him out?"

"You really trust that little bastard?"

"I like him."

"I think you're a bad judge of character, but pay the clerk $18 for the bottle and $50 for his processing fee. I'll look for a call from you tomorrow, right?"

"Right," Brett said.

A police car drove them back to the St. Regis and both men were careful not to discuss anything related to the kidnap. When they were safely in their room Brett turned to Manny, "Where the hell is the bag with the two million?"

"On the chair in the corner," Manny replied, with a grin.

Brett looked toward the corner. "How... how the hell did you do that?"

"Pour me a drink from the bar and I'll tell you." Manny replied.

Brett emptied four miniatures of Chivas Regal into two glasses and they sat down at the desk. Manny took a slug and said, "The locker was a decoy, I knew they'd go straight for it. There was a courier service, Manhattan Express, inside the station. I made sure the satchel was locked and I had them box it for me. I paid them to deliver it to the St. Regis with instructions to send it to your room."

Brett just stared at him in astonishment. "You trusted two million dollars to a courier?"

"Had to. If the police got hold of two million in funny money, we go to jail for a long time. Besides, the guy looked honest."

Brett downed a gulp of Scotch, looked at Manny, and then coughed up the liquor through his nose as they both starting laughing.

CHAPTER TWENTY-EIGHT

New York City, N.Y.
September 7, 2001

9:45 p.m.

Pat O'Hara and Al Czychowitz were exhausted. They had rushed home from California, staked out the arrival of Brett and Manny, arrested them, then released them, and in the end had very little new information regarding the killing in the Times Square Hotel a week ago.

"Cup a Coffee?" Al asked.

"Why not, might as well make it an even dozen."

Al slipped out to the coffee room and returned with two quasi white mugs with the name Beltramo Bail Bonds inscribed on them. It appeared as if they hadn't been washed since they were first donated to the precinct a year ago. Al set them down on Pat's desk blotter. "What's your take?" he said.

"On Raven and his buddy or on the murder?"

"Both, they're somehow related."

Ignoring the handle, Pat palmed the cup with his meaty hand and pressed it to his lips. "They're both a lot smarter than we thought. I have no idea how that Manny guy got rid of the satchel and it's obvious Raven is clever enough not to give up any information unless it helps him on his mission."

"What is his mission?" Al asked.

"It has to be a kidnap and that missing case must have the ransom in it. It's just odd that Raven thinks he can handle it himself rather than bringing in the police."

"Maybe his wife did pull the trigger and he's afraid she'll face a charge."

"That doesn't fit real well. If she's the victim, why would he think she'd be charged for killing her captor?"

Al ran his fingers through the front of his hair and scratched his scalp. "We're at a disadvantage. There's some ugly history involved between all these people; we just don't know what it is."

Pat looked at Al as if he had just had an epiphany. "Al, I think you hit on it. Raven wants his wife back but has some shit he has to hide. He's a pretty cocky guy and probably figures he can pull it off and still keep some ugly secrets buried."

"You think he plans to just exchange the money for his wife, or do you think he has Manny with him to deliver some payback after the payoff?"

"Not sure, what did the background check on Manny show?"

"A couple arrests, mostly minor, except for one ten years ago for beating the shit out of a guy in a bar. Looks like he works as kind of an enforcer for some small time gangster in the Bay Area."

"Strange friendship," Pat said. "A respected health professional and a petty gangster."

"Let's look at the main players again," Al said. "Talbot, who supposedly died in a plane crash, was married to Raven's ex-wife. Erskine investigates insurance fraud and ends up partners with the guy he probably was stalking. Raven re-marries his ex-wife after Talbot is declared dead, and Manny is Raven's good friend who watches his back side like a brother."

"Someone else is in this web," Pat said. "With one player dead and only one left, this kidnap deal couldn't go down. Can't watch the hostage and pick up the ransom at the same time."

"We have to be there when the exchange takes place, then we can nail the remaining kidnappers and we'll have our killer."

Pat reflected on Al's statement. "How do we tail Raven and his buddy? They spotted us pretty easily on the way back from Teterboro?"

Al had another epiphany. "Did they release that weasel Clemente yet?"

"Why?" Pat asked.

"I think those guys want to use him for surveillance or something like that. I don't think they sprung him out of the goodness of their hearts."

"Let's go," Pat said.

The holding cell was two floors down and in the adjoining building. Both detectives broke into a jog and Al reached the desk first. "Is Clemente still here?" he asked the sergeant in charge.

"Just left about two minutes ago, you may be able to catch him," the guard replied.

This time Pat emptied his lungs at full speed and popped through the exit door; Cam was there leaning against the building and lighting up a cigarette. "Come back in for a minute, Cam, we have to talk."

"Shit man, I'm paid up, I'm out," Cam replied.

"Looks like you may be a suspect on another charge," Pat said. "Cuffs or no cuffs?"

Cam took a puff on his cigarette and then in disgust, threw it on the sidewalk and stamped it out with his scuffed shoe. "This is bullshit, just bullshit, isn't it? You don't have another charge, do you?'

"Come on in, we'll see."

Cam went ahead of the detective kicking the floor as he walked. "Bullshit, this is bullshit."

"Have a seat," Pat said, as they entered a stark interrogation room where Al was already seated at a rickety wooden table surrounded by four card table chairs.

"Hey Cam," Al said.

"Fu…fuck you," Cam replied.

"Is that how your mommy taught you to talk?" Al laughed.

"You ain't my mommy, ass… asshole."

Pat took a seat at the table. "Okay, Cam, let's cut to the chase. What did those guys offer you?"

"What guys?"

Al swiped the back of his hand against Cam's right cheek. "It's late and I want to go home. Just answer the question."

Cam gently rubbed his fingers over the side of his face. "Don't have to get nasty," he said.

"The question, Cam, answer the question."

"They offered me a grand to help 'em. Didn't say what I'd have to do."

"How you supposed to get together?" Al asked.

"I'm supposed to call Raven at the St. Regis tomorrow morning."

"Okay," Al said. "You work for us now, understand?"

"Come on guys, I need that grand, I'm broke."

"Play this right and they'll pay you the grand, we'll get our information and we'll get off your back."

Cam looked down at the leather peeling off the end of his shoes. "I really need that money," he said softly to the detective.

"I told you, work with us and you'll get it."

Cam knew he was beaten. "Okay, what do I need to do?"

Chapter Twenty-Nine

New York City, N.Y.
September 7, 2001

11:15 p.m.

It was over two hours since they had been released from jail and Brett was edgy waiting for some contact from the kidnappers. "Stop pacing the floor and take it easy on the booze," Manny said. "They'll call."

"I know, just nervous."

Manny pointed to the room service tray that had been delivered twenty minutes ago. "Eat something; it'll clear the Scotch out of your system."

Brett picked up a crisp french fry and ran it through a mound of ketchup. As he was stuffing it into his mouth, his cell buzzed twice. He looked over at Manny. "Remember the terms we talked about," Manny said.

Brett nodded and flipped open the lid of his Motorola. "Raven."

The distorted voice came through in a monotone. "Who answered your phone a few hours ago?"

"A cop," Brett replied.

"Are you crazy, we said no cops if you want to see Annie alive."

"Yeah, well, it wasn't by choice, they arrested me at the airport. Seems someone got killed in a hotel room and they think it has something to do with Annie. Does it?"

There was silence from the other end of the phone until finally the voice said, "Your wife is safe, that's all you need to know. What did you tell the police?"

"Nothing, but they're not stupid. They know I'm here for a reason."

"What about the money? Did they find it?"

"Give me a little credit. I want Annie back, and the money is safe."

"Are they still following you?"

"Probably, but I can lose them. I have help."

"Help, what help?" the voice asked.

"A loan broker from Palm Beach. You may have met him." Brett replied.

After a brief pause the caller said, "I don't know what you're talking about. Just keep him out of the way."

"Don't worry, he's here to make sure you get the money and I get Annie."

"Okay, let's talk about the exchange."

"Whoa," Brett said. "You know the deal, I want proof Annie is safe before I give you my life savings."

"I told you she was safe."

"And why would I believe a turd like you. I want a photo of her and I want her holding up the front page of tomorrow's New York Times."

The phone went silent again, but Brett thought he could hear a muffled conversation in the background. Finally the voice droned back, "Okay, how will we get it to you?"

Brett plucked an information card off the desk. "The hotel has a fax service; the number is 555-2700. Use a cover page: Attention Dr. Raven."

"Okay, but have the money ready for delivery," the voice said, and the phone went dead.

"You did good, real good," Manny said.

"Thanks, what's next?"

"I'm goin' down to the lobby to pick up a few things. Give housekeeping a call and tell them we don't want our room made up during our stay."

Brett scratched his head. "Whatever," he said.

Manny was gone for twenty minutes and returned with a little bag from the hotel shop. "Looks like you're a big shopper," Brett said.

Manny laughed, "Yeah, a real shopaholic," he replied, as he took a package of single edge razor blades and a roll of packing tape out of the plastic sack. "Help me strip one of these beds."

They each grabbed one side of the quilt and pulled it off the foot of the bed and then dumped the sheets on top of it. Manny unwrapped one of the blades and sliced through the mattress making a two foot cross. "Give me one of those sheets," he instructed Brett.

Brett yanked a sheet out of the pile and laid it on the floor beside the bed. Manny began removing the stuffing from the mattress and throwing it onto the open sheet. "Come on, give me a hand."

They both pulled and twisted until there was a large cavity where the stuffing used to be. "Toss me the satchel," Manny said, as he patted down the bottom of the hole.

Brett brought the leather case over and unlocked it. Manny began unloading the money and said, "Should fit pretty well in here." One by one he stacked the packets edge to edge and top to bottom until the entire forty-four and a half pounds of money filled the void. "Do we have a thick bath mat," he asked.

Brett went to the bathroom, returned with the mat and handed it to Manny who was taping the slits closed with packing tape; he laid the mat over the repaired incisions. "Okay, let's re-make it."

When the bed was back to looking normal,

Brett said, "I called housekeeping; no maid service for us this week.

"Perfect," Manny said, as he rolled up the sheet full of stuffing, slung it over his shoulder and headed toward the door. "When I get back we'll flip a coin to see who sleeps on two million dollars tonight."

CHAPTER THIRTY

New York City, N.Y.
September 8, 2001

8:15 a.m.

"Phone's ringing," Manny yelled from the bathroom.

Brett looked at his watch, 8:15. "Raven," he said.

"Hey, Brett, it's me, me Cam. You guys told me to call ya, member?"

"Sure, Cam. You're right on time. Any problems getting out of jail last night?"

"No, it was easy, real easy. Thanks to you guys it was a piece of cake. You still think you'll have some, you know, work for me?"

"Had breakfast yet?" Brett asked.

"Had a beer, but no food."

"Know where the St. Regis is?"

Cam laughed. "I know where it is, but never been there. A little, you know, uptown for me."

"Meet us in the coffee shop next to the lobby at nine."

"Okay, but I'm a little short on cash. Do I have to tip or anything to get in the door?"

"Just walk right in. See you in forty-five minutes."

Brett picked a table in the back of the restaurant, ordered a cup of coffee, and began perusing the Times while he waited for Manny to join him. The headline read **FAILED UNION NEGOTIATIONS THREATEN GARBAGE COLLECTION**. In the lower right side of the same page a smaller headline read **Greenwich Village Comedy Club Burns Down**. The lower left featured another article, **Subway Train Stopped Over an Hour**. He ignored all of them and went to the editorial page in search of a more interesting story. Before he could find one, he heard a voice say, "Hey, man, nice place."

Brett looked up. "Hi, Cam, take a seat."

"Thanks, thanks, nice place, real nice."

"Coffee?" Brett asked.

Cam wrinkled his nose. "Think they'll make a Bloody Mary this early?"

Brett laughed and said, "You're going to have to do something about your diet. You're missing a few of the food groups."

"Don't get it," Cam replied.

"Never mind, I'm sure you can get a drink."

Manny sauntered in ten minutes later and took the third seat at the table. "Well, well, if it's not the Puerto Rican chameleon. How ya doin', Cam?"

"Doin' good, doin' good. How you doin'?"

"Perfect," Manny said, looking at Cam's Bloody Mary. "How 'bout breakfast, something without alcohol maybe?"

Brett ordered oatmeal and Manny French Toast. Cam shocked them by ordering Eggs Benedict. "I'm surprised," Brett said. "You didn't strike me as an Eggs Benedict kind of guy."

Cam finished off his Bloody Mary. "Never had 'em, but that yellow Holidays Sauce looked good."

"Did those detectives give you a hard time after we left?" Manny asked.

"What detectives?" Cam replied.

Manny looked at Brett who rolled his eyes and said, "You do remember being in a cell with us right?"

"Yeah, sure, yeah. Oh, those detectives. No problem, didn't even see 'em again."

"Why you so nervous?" Manny asked.

"Me? I'm not nervous, I'm always like this. Just excited about making some money. What's the deal, what's the deal."

"Just relax, Brett said. "We'll fill you in when the time is right. We can trust you, correct?"

A little bead of sweat appeared on Cam's upper lip. "Trust me, trust me? Shit yeah," he answered. "Why you ask that?"

Manny edged closer to Cam and put his face in his, "We told you mob money is in this deal. If you cross us you're dead meat."

Cam wiped his lip with his shirt sleeve. "Don't worry, don't worry, you can trust me."

"I hope so, for your sake, I hope so." Manny said.

Brett looked at his watch again, 9:55. "I'll check on that fax, be right back," he said to Manny as he pushed his chair back.

Cam was still working on the eggs and having a hard time getting the rich creamy sauce past his tongue. As he picked at the edges, Manny slapped the fork against the plate knocking it out of his hand. "The fuck," Cam said. "Why'd you do that?"

"I got a bad feeling about you this morning Cam. I got a feeling you don't have our best interests at heart."

"What cha mean? I need the money. I'll do anything you ask."

"Will you double cross those detectives?"

Cam started to sweat again and his hand began to quiver. "Don't know what cha mean."

Manny pushed Cam's plate to the end of the table and honed in on him. "I think you do, they threatened you didn't they?"

"Who?"

"The cops, Cam, the cops."

Cam shrunk down in his chair. "I wouldn't have done it, honest. I told 'em I'd help 'em but I was goin' to tell you, honest."

"Like when, after you back-stabbed us?"

"Cam turned pale and he grabbed his stomach. "I gotta puke, the eggs are coming up?"

"I'll give you five minutes in the head, and then get back in here."

Cam pushed his chair back and ran for the bathroom passing Brett on the way. What's his problem?" Brett asked, as he sat back down and threw two pieces of paper on the table.

"Cam is trying to come to grips with reality."

"Meaning?" Brett asked.

"Meaning, the cops turned him. He's a spy."

"So what do we do with him?"

"Turn him back around," Manny replied. "Got the fax?"

Brett flipped the first piece of shiny paper face up. There was Annie looking back at them. Her hair was flat, she had what appeared to be a cold sore on her upper lip and she looked pale, but surprisingly she didn't look scared. She was holding the front page of the New York Times. "You okay?" Manny asked.

"Yeah, I'm okay, but I want to get those bastards."

"Maybe, maybe not, let's remember our mission: get Annie back."

Brett nodded, picked up the fax and zeroed in on it to get a better look. "What do you see?" Manny asked.

Brett looked closer, scrutinizing the picture of Annie holding the newspaper. "Look at Annie's fingers."

Manny took the paper from Brett and concentrated his gaze on Annie's hand positions. Her right hand was holding up that side of the newspaper and four fingers were visible. Her left hand was supporting the other side, but instead of displaying four fingers, only her index finger was visible and it was pointing straight down to the first words of the small headline; **Greenwich Village Comedy C...** "You thinking what I'm thinking?" Manny asked.

"She's being held somewhere in Greenwich Village," Brett replied.

Cam slithered back to the table looking white as a sheet. He had obviously lost his first bout with Eggs Benedict. "Sit down and keep your mouth shut," Manny commanded. Cam obeyed and slumped into a chair.

Brett ignored Cam and picked up the cover sheet

of the two page fax. He reached for his reading glasses and held the paper toward the light coming from the overhead hanging lamp. "Take a look at this one," Brett said to Manny.

Manny squinted at the page but saw nothing other than ATTENTION: DR. RAVEN.

"What?" he asked.

"Look at the bottom of the page. It's very faint, almost like a watermark."

Manny looked again. "I see something but can't make it out."

Brett handed him his readers and Manny placed them on his nose. "K-I-N-K-O-S," he spelled out loud.

"I'll check the yellow pages," Brett said, as he jumped up and headed for the lobby.

Manny looked at Cam who was cowering in his chair. "We're goin' to see the man." Manny said.

"What, what man?"

"The boss man," Manny replied.

"No please, I don't wanta' see the boss man. Let me help you guys, please. You don't even have to pay me. Please, I don't want the mob after me."

"What will you tell the detectives when they get a hold of you?"

"I'll lie; I'm good at it, sometimes. You tell me what to say and I'll say it."

Manny didn't respond as he saw Brett returning

to the table. "Find it?" Manny asked.

"Yeah, there're only four Kinko's in the city and one is in Greenwich Village on 8th near Bleeker."

Manny turned toward Cam who was still pale and trembling. "You want a second chance?"

Cam sat up as if coming to attention in a parade line. "Yeah, yeah, please. I won't let ya down."

Manny looked at Brett who nodded his head. "Okay, Chameleon, we're going to see if you can do what you claim you can do or if you're just full of shit. If you come through for us in the next few days, you'll get your grand; otherwise kiss your ass goodbye."

"You won't be sorry," Cam replied with a sigh of relief.

Brett took out a piece of paper and wrote down the address of Kinkos along with the fax number for the hotel. "You've got a half hour to get down there. Keep an eye on the fax station. The guy you're looking for is going to fax this number, 555-2700. Follow that guy back to an apartment or wherever he goes."

"Got it, got it," Cam said.

"You have a cell phone?" Manny asked.

"Yeah, yeah, I got one."

"Where the hell did you get a cell phone?" Manny said.

"Borrowed it."

"From who?"

"Electronics store on 44th."

Brett took back the paper he had given Cam and jotted a number down. "This is my cell, call as soon as you have something."

"I will, honest, I won't disappoint you guys," he said, as he jumped off his chair.

Brett reached in his pocket and took out a bill. "Here's a twenty, take a cab."

As soon as Cam was out of sight, Manny asked, "How you going to get them to go back to Kinkos?"

"This fax is so blurry I can't make out the date on the newspaper, can you?"

Manny smiled, "It really is blurry, isn't it? Guess they'll have to send a new one."

CHAPTER THIRTY-ONE

11:30 a.m.

"Sleep good?" O'Hara asked.

"Ten hours straight through," Al replied. "You?"

"Good," he said, as he glanced at his wrist. "Shit it's after eleven already. Should we check on our boy?"

"Go ahead, but he's probably hung over somewhere."

Pat flipped through the favorite numbers on his phone. When Cam's name came up he hit dial and waited. The phone rang six times before the call was picked up, "Angel Clemente speaking."

"Hello, Mr. Clemente, I was expecting your secretary to answer."

"Who's this?" Cam asked.

"You know who it is, asshole. Where are you?"

"I'm running an errand for the guys."

"What kind of errand?"

"Uh, they said they had a lead on someone in Harlem. I'm in a cab on my way up there to check it out."

"Isn't that where your mother lives?"

"Keep my mother out'a this. She'd kill me if she knew I was a stool pigeon for cops."

"Okay, forget I said that. What're those guys up to?"

"Hell if I know. Raven gave me twenty bucks and said, "Go check out the Kinko's in Harlem.""

"Check it out for what?"

"He, he got a fax from up there. Wants me to look out for a guy."

"What guy?"

"I don't know," he just said, "look out for a guy who faxes the St.Regis."

"You have my number?' Pat asked.

"Yeah, sure, I got it."

"You call me if you spot the guy, understand?"

"Sure, sure I understand."

"By the way, can you get inside their room?"

"Their room? Why would I want to get inside their room?"

"Because I want you to, that's why."

"Oh, sure, I can probably get in there."

"Okay, get in there and see if you spot a leather

satchel. I want to know what's inside it."

"That it?" Cam finally asked.

"Call me this afternoon and have something to tell me, understand?"

"Yeah, yeah I understand."

Czychowitz had been listening to only one side of the conversation, but was pretty sure he understood it. "Trust him?"

O'Hara pondered the question. "I don't know, maybe."

The cab dropped Cam off in Greenwich Village at the corner of Hudson and Eighth and he walked a block over to Bleeker St. where he spotted the big blue K on the building as soon as he turned the corner.

The Chameleon walked through the automatic front door and immediately knew he was in strange territory; he had never been in a store before that didn't have something he might want to steal. It made him nervous and he started mumbling to himself, "Don't screw this up, don't screw this up."

"May I help you?" A plump young girl dressed in a red and blue uniform asked.

"Uh, just lookin' around. May need to send a fax later though. Uh, how do I do that?"

"I can show you. It's in the back of the store."

Cam fell in step behind the clerk, keeping his

eyes on her bouncing chubby buns as she led him to the rear of the room. "Here we are," she said, turning back in his direction.

He had no idea what the machines sitting on the long white Formica counter were for. "Thanks, yeah, thanks a lot. Uh, which one's the fax?"

"Have you ever used a fax?" the clerk asked.

"Sure, but it's been a while," he lied.

The young girl pointed to a gray box with a keyboard on its face. "This is it," she said. "Just put the document you want to fax in the top tray and use the keyboard to dial the number where you're sending it. Then push O.K."

"How do I check to make sure I'm dialing the right number?"

The clerk set her puffy index finger on a screen. "It shows up right here, just check it before you push O.K."

"Wow, cool. Thanks, thanks a lot," Cam said.

"No problem. Anything else I can help with?"

"Uh yeah, you think you'd like to grab a beer with me sometime, maybe?"

The clerk's face flushed. "I don't think so," she said, as she shuffled back toward the front of the store.

Cam didn't blend well in this store, he had the feeling he looked like a lemon in a case of oranges. Trying desperately not to attract attention, he casually strolled out the front door, leaned against a no parking sign, and lit up a cigarette. He watched intently as customers entered and left the building.

The Copy Center was in the back of the store; however, he had direct line of sight to it from the position he had taken up out front. His first hit was a short bald headed man who, after entering, headed straight for the rear of the store. Cam threw his cigarette on the sidewalk and crushed it under his scuffed shoe, then quickly followed the man to the back. The short guy didn't even look at the fax machine as he disappeared into the men's room.

Cam retreated to his surveillance position, but before he could light up again, another man entered the store and walked to the rear. This time Cam made sure the man stopped at the Fax before he hustled inside and approached the gray machine. The man was tapping in a number on the keyboard. "Hey," Cam said.

The man looked up, "Oh, hi, you waiting for this machine?"

"No, uh, ah, just trying to figure out how that keyboard works."

The guy laughed, "Pretty easy," he said. "Take a peek." Cam squeezed in just close enough to where he could make out the screen. He was looking for 2700 as the last four digits dialed, but none of those numbers were on the screen. "Oh, I see. Does look easy, thanks," he said, and made his way back to the front.

Three cigarettes and forty-five minutes later he spotted another customer moving in the direction of the fax. By the time he reached the machine the phone number had already been punched in. "S'cuse me, did you find a paper in that top tray? I just sent a fax and I think I left it there."

The fax user looked around. "Don't see anything."

Cam feigned concern as he moved his gaze over the screen and caught sight of 5-2700. "Sorry, must have dropped it on my way out," he said.

His hands were shaking as he dialed Brett's cell number. "Raven," a voice echoed through the receiver.

"Brett, it's me Cam."

"I just received the fax, are you following the person who sent it?"

"Can't."

"Why?"

"Sped off in a cab."

"So why didn't you follow?"

"Only have four bucks left from the twenty."

Brett was kicking himself for not giving Cam some extra money. "Did you get a good look at him?" he asked.

"Not a him," he replied

"What do you mean?"

"Wasn't a guy, it was a woman."

"What do you mean a woman?"

"You know what a woman is, long blonde hair, nice legs, big tits."

Brett, nonplussed, stared into space. "Come on back to the hotel," he said, as he shut the cover of his flip top phone.

THE PAYOFF

9/8/01 – 9/12/01

Chapter Thirty-Two

New York City, N.Y.
September 8, 2001

5:00 p.m.

Brett answered his cell on the first ring and heard the slurred voice coming through the receiver. "Did the second fax come through?" it asked.

"Yes, I got it," he answered, while looking down at the picture of Annie holding the morning copy of the New York Times.

"Are you convinced your wife is safe and sound?"

"She looks safe but not very sound."

"Sorry we didn't bring in a cosmetologist. You want her back or not?"

"Of course I want her back."

"Okay, here's what you do. Make sure the money's in a case with a handle and take it to the 51st. St. subway station, about four blocks from your hotel, tonight before 8 p.m. Buy a ticket on the #6 line going south and get on the train that arrives in the station at 8:11. Sit on the left side, in the first row of the last car. Did you hear that?"

"Yeah, I heard it: #6 south, 8:11, left side, first row, last car. Then what?"

"Put the case under the seat and get off the train at the next stop, 42nd St."

"That it?"

"That's it," the monotonous voice answered.

"I think you forgot something."

"What's that?"

"How do I get Annie?"

"We'll call you with an address after we get the money and you can go and pick her up."

"Hold it," Brett said in an excited voice. "That wasn't the deal."

"Golden rule. We have your golden girl so we make the rules."

Brett had his cell on speaker and looked toward Manny who was monitoring the conversation. Manny gave him a thumbs down. "No way," Brett said.

"You don't have a choice Raven. #6, 8:11, don't be late." The phone went dead.

Brett closed the lid of his cell. "What do you think?" he said, turning to Manny.

"Tough call, if it were my money I wouldn't give it to 'em, but if it were my wife I probably would."

Brett sat in silence for several minutes and then said, "Let's give them half. That'll at least insure Annie's safety until they get the other half."

Manny thought about it. "That's not a bad idea. Those greedy bastards won't be happy with only half a pie," he said, as he began stripping the bed.

Brett grabbed the leather case and brought it over to Manny who was carefully counting out the packets of money which were buried in the mattress. One by one he passed them to Brett. "Hundred ninety-nine, two hundred," Manny mumbled, as he passed the last two bundles of bills to him. "That's the first installment, one million."

Brett neatly piled the packages of cash into the case and clicked the clasp shut. "Cam's having a beer in the lounge. I'll get him up here; looks like we're going to need him."

"I'm sure the other people at the bar will thank you."

Responding to the knock, Manny opened the door. "Hey, man, how you doin"? Cam said as he slithered into the room.

"Doin' good, Brett has a new job for you."

Cam gave a quick look around the room and spied the leather satchel resting on the desk chair. He looked away from the desk and greeted Brett. "I'm ready for more work, I'm ready. What's the deal?"

"Good, you see that case over there?" Brett said, nodding toward the desk.

Cam looked in the direction Brett indicated and pretended to see the satchel for the first time. "The brown leather one?"

"Yes, Cam, the brown leather one. The only one in the room."

"Sure, sure, want me to deliver it somewhere?"

"No, but I want you to be able to recognize it."

"Okay, no problem," Cam said, as he stared at the case.

Brett snapped his fingers and Cam took his gaze off the satchel. "Concentrate on what I'm going to tell you. You can't screw this up, you hear?"

"I'm good, what?"

"I want you to go down to the Bleeker St. Subway Station. Know where it is?"

"You kidding, I've lived in this City almost all my life. The station is right near that Kinko's store you sent me to."

"I know, that's why you're going to that station. I want you to be next to the tracks at 8:15. A couple minutes later a southbound #6 will roll in. Zero in on the last car and look for someone coming out carrying this case."

"Okay, then what?"

"Go into your chameleon mode and follow that

person and don't get spotted. I want to know where this case ends up."

"I'm cool, I'm cool. What's in the case?"

"You're on a need to know basis, only when I need you to know. Right now you don't need to know."

"No problemo. Hey, you guys hungry? I'm starved."

Manny took a pair of twenties out of his pocket, looked at his watch, and handed the bills to Cam. "It's 6:10, you've got two hours. Buy yourself some dinner, but be at that station a half hour early."

Cam stuffed the bills into his pocket. "I'm on it. Want me to call you or bring the info back?"

"Call," Brett said.

"Okay, by the way, I have a new phone."

"Why?" Manny asked.

"Company disconnected the old one. Picked up a better model."

Brett smiled for the first time since getting the ransom call. "Emphasis on 'picked up,'" he said.

The humor wasn't lost on Cam. "Whatever works, talk to you guys later," he said, as he headed for the door while checking his pocket to make sure the bills were still there.

Cam made a bee line for the coffee shop next to the lobby where he ordered a filet mignon and a pitcher of Bud. When he had drained the pitcher, he belched for the third time and looked at his watch. "Oh, shit," he said, to himself as he grabbed the check and sprinted to the cashier. He added a generous tip, signed Brett's name and room number, and hailed a cab outside the front entrance. "Bleeker St. Station and make it as fast as you can," he said, while waving a twenty dollar bill in the direction of the cab driver.

The taxi pulled up to the subway entrance and Cam looked at the meter. It only read twelve dollars and change, but he reluctantly dropped the twenty onto the front seat and ran down the steps taking two at a time. He looked at the large digital clock display next to the train schedule; it read 8:17 and as he looked up, he heard the sound of a train accelerating out of the station. He caught a peek at its number. It was the #6.

A wave of panic overtook him and he thought he would vomit until he turned toward the escalator and caught a glimpse of the brown satchel swinging next to a great pair of legs as it disappeared from the top step onto the street. He vaulted up the moving stairs and onto the sidewalk, but the only person he saw within twenty yards was a homeless guy with a sign that read "God Bless." He looked up and down Bleeker, but no sign of the case; then he looked down Lafayette and caught sight of the woman with the satchel waiting for the light to change at Houston St. He fell into step fifty yards behind and followed her two blocks down Mulberry where she disappeared into an entryway. By the time he caught up, all he found was a locked door leading into a rundown brick building, **#276 Mulberry Arms Apartments**

"It was the same broad, the good looker from Kinko's," Cam said, as Brett listened to his report.

"Where did she go?"

"Somewhere on Mulberry."

"You have the address?"

"Don't have it. She disappeared into one of the buildings before I could catch up to her."

Brett was disappointed. "Okay, good job," he said. "Meet us for breakfast tomorrow at eight."

CHAPTER THIRTY-THREE

8:30 a.m.

Cam was looking forward to a plate of good old fashion bacon and eggs. The last time he had breakfast with the guys at the St. Regis, he had ordered a fancy dish and had thrown it up all over the marble floor of the men's room. He smiled knowing that last night, even though he had almost blown it, he still managed to come up with valuable information, only some of which he shared with Brett. As he turned the corner onto 55th, a black Ford sedan screeched to a halt right next to him. Cam looked to his left just in time to see Czychowitz emerging from the front passenger door, which set him into his imitation of the hundred yard dash.

Track was never one of Cam's best sports; in fact Cam didn't have any best sports. In high school he usually smoked cigarettes under the bleachers while the jocks, few of whom he even knew, were practicing sports on the nearby fields. The detective caught up to him within ten yards of chase and grabbed his arm. "Where you going in such a hurry, buddy?" Al asked.

"Oh, Detective C, didn't see ya there. What's doin'?"

"What's doing? What the hell do you think is doing? Your phone is disconnected and you haven't checked in with us." The detective pushed him toward the Ford which had motored up next to them. "Get in," he said.

"Sure, sure, don't get so excited," Cam replied, as he slid onto the back seat with Czychowitz squeezing in next to him.

"Well, well, if it isn't the Puerto Rican flash," O'Hara said, from the front seat. "You trying to run away from us?"

Cam feigned ignorance. "Me? No, I was just in a hurry."

"A hurry? A hurry to get where?" Al asked. "You have a big social life now?"

Cam knew he was busted and tried to wriggle out of it. "Okay, I apologize, I should have called, but I'm in tight with these guys. I'm getting all the shit you want to know. I was goin' to call you right after I had breakfast with 'em."

"I'll bet you were," Al said. "Let's talk now

instead."

"Sure, sure, what d' you want to know?"

"Did you see the satchel we were talking about?"

"Yeah, they did a drop on the subway. Gorgeous blonde picked it up."

"What was in it?"

"I don't know, but I'm guessing it wasn't full of dirty socks."

"Did you see any cash?"

Cam fiddled with a cigarette. "Mind if I smoke?" he asked, and then lit up before an answer was forthcoming. "I didn't see any cash, but I'm sure there was a lot of it in there. Those guys were talking about two million when we were in the cage."

"Where was the drop?" Al asked.

"On the subway, number six southbound."

"Where is it now?" Pat asked.

Cam took a long drag on the Newport. "I love menthol, don't you? Cleans out the sinuses," he said, as he exhaled a big puff of smoke.

"I don't smoke," Pat said, thinking about the bet with his wife. "Where is it now? I asked you."

Cam couldn't figure out a good lie so went briefly with the truth. "It's in Greenwich Village somewhere."

"What d'ya mean, somewhere?" Czychowitz said.

"I followed the babe who was carrying it, but she slipped away on Mulberry."

"Where about's on Mulberry?" Pat asked.

"Don't know exactly. Followed her from the Bleeker St. Station but she gave me the slip just after Houston."

"Why do I think you're lying to us?" Pat said.

"I'm not shittin' ya, honest, that's what happened."

Al took hold of the front of Cam's shirt and pressed him against the back seat. "Okay, buddy, listen, and listen good. Two guys nabbed Raven's wife in California and brought her here to New York. That woman you followed was the courier to transport the ransom money. We don't give a shit about the kidnap since Raven thinks he's smart enough to handle it on his own and won't take any help, but one of those kidnappers is dead and we're going to get the killer. If you jack us around, we'll get you on an obstructing justice charge and you'll go down as an accomplice to the murder."

Cam had the taste of stomach acid reach his tongue. "What d' ya need to keep me out of this? I'm getting in over my head."

"Just keep playing along with Raven and his buddy. They're going to figure out where the wife is, and when they do you're going to tell us. The killer is with her and we want him."

"Good, I'm good with it, just cut me some slack. If they find out I'm helping you they'll throw me to Manny's mob."

"I doubt Manny is part of the mob," Czychowitz said with a smirk.

"Yeah, well where else would two million dollars come from? Just give me some space and I'll call ya as soon as I have an address."

Al let go of Cam's shirt and reached into his own pants pocket. "Here's a key card to Raven's hotel room, we want you to sneak in there and look around. We don't have a warrant, just a key, so we can't do it, but since you found that key on the floor, nothings stopping you."

Cam took the key. "Okay," he said reluctantly, and stuffed it into his pocket. "How do I get a chance? They seem to be headquartering in there."

"We'll make sure you have a window, just don't cross us or we'll put your balls in a blender and push chop."

"I get it, okay, I get it," Cam said, as he put the cigarette out between the floor carpet and his shoe. "I'll call."

Al opened the door and stepped out to give room for Cam to make his exit. "Have a nice breakfast," he said, as he gave Cam a kiss on the forehead.

CHAPTER THIRTY-FOUR

New York City, N.Y.
September 9, 2001

9:00 a.m.

Brett and Manny were already eating by the time Cam made it to the hotel coffee shop. He came bouncing past the hostess like a rap singer taking the stage. "What's doin'?" he said.

Both men looked up and nodded, and Brett gestured toward a chair. "Anything new?'" he asked.

"What can be new? I lost the chick and the ransom money on Mulberry and then headed home."

Manny looked up abruptly from his food. "Ransom money? Who said anything about ransom money?"

The color seemed to drain from Cam's face. "Yo… you did or Brett did."

Before Cam could answer, he was saved by the

waitress who arrived at the table and asked for his order. "Bacon n' eggs over easy," he replied. Not willing to make eye contact, he poured himself some coffee and took his time adding sugar and stirring it around as if he had a secret recipe, then he spooned a taste into his mouth, licked his lips and said, "Ahh."

Manny leaned over and closed in, Cam could smell the Chorizo from the breakfast burrito on his breath. "We never said anything about ransom money," Manny said.

"Well, I guess I just figured that was what was in the satchel."

"Why would you figure that?" Brett asked.

"I just figured, that's all."

"Who you been talkin' to?" Manny asked.

"No one. Who would I talk to?"

"I'm thinking Detective O'Hara and Detective Czychowitz," Brett said.

"You kiddin'?" He replied, as his breakfast was set on the table by the waitress. "Why would I talk to those pricks?"

"Because you haven't decided which side you're on. Which is it Cam, the cops or us?" Manny asked.

"I'm with you, honest. Those dicks told me Raven's wife was kidnapped, so I figured the drop on the subway was ransom money, but I wouldn't lend a hand to them guys if they was drowning."

There was silence except for the sound of Cam slurping up the eggs. Finally, Brett broke it, "We want you to watch that area on Mulberry. We have to know which apartment house that woman went into. Can we trust you to do that and not tell the cops?"

"Absolutely," Cam replied, as he ate a piece of bacon with his fingers.

Brett was just about to finish giving Cam his assignment when a voice behind him bellowed out. "Well, well, the Tooth Doc, the Mob Boss, and the Chameleon, all having a cozy breakfast together. Since when have you guys been such good friends?" Czychowitz asked.

Manny looked over his shoulder at the detectives. "Since the sleep-over at your place. Found out the three of us have a lot in common."

"I'll bet. I'm sure you're discussing common views on world peace. Get lost," he said, looking directly at Cam.

Cam looked at Manny. "See ya later," Manny said to him, waving his hand toward the exit.

"Yeah, see ya," Cam said, as he stuffed two pieces of toast into his pocket and headed toward the lobby.

"Mind if we join you?" O'Hara asked.

"Delighted," Brett replied.

The detectives sat down and poured themselves

coffee from the ceramic pot sitting in the middle of the table. "How 'bout we show you ours, then you show us yours?" Czychowitz said.

"I hope we're talking about information," Brett replied.

O'Hara laughed and moved his chair closer to Brett. "Raven, we've figured out why you're here and what you're up to."

"What am I up to?" Brett asked.

"Your wife was kidnapped by a couple guys who for some reason don't like you very much and think they're entitled to your money. You brought it, lots of it like $2 million, to New York to get her back."

"Suppose you're right, why do you even care? Is crime actually so slow in Manhattan that you have to spend time helping people who don't want your help?" Brett said.

Czychowitz joined in. "We don't really give a shit if you get your wife back or not; all we care about is solving a murder case that our lieutenant wants solved. Then we get a pat on the back and a gold star on our record and maybe a chance at early retirement. You see Raven, it's all about us, not about you."

"What do you want from me?" Brett asked.

"We want to know where they're keeping her."

"I want to know that too."

"But you're close and we're not," O'Hara added.

"How 'bout we work together?"

Manny who had remained silent through the conversation said, "Give us some time to talk it over."

"This prick talk for you?" Czychowitz said, turning toward Brett.

Brett looked him in the eyes, "Yeah, Al, he does, and if you even want me to consider your offer, you better apologize to Manny here."

Czychowitz looked as if the top of his head was going to blow off. "I'm not apologizing to some two bit hood."

Brett looked at O'Hara. "Apologize," O'Hara said to his partner.

Czychowitz jumped up off his chair and stomped out of the coffee shop. "Give him a minute," Pat said.

Brett refilled all the cups and the three of them sat silently drinking coffee. Five minutes later Czychowitz reappeared at the table, took a gulp of caffeine, and turned toward Manny. "Sorry," he said, with more than a hint of insincerity.

"No problem," Manny replied, picking up the conversation from where it had left off. "Brett and I will talk it over. How do we get a hold of you?"

Pat reached into his pocket for a card and handed it to Manny. "Call anytime, but the sooner the better. We've got a feeling your money and our killer won't be hanging around too much longer."

"The kidnappers said no cops," Brett replied.

"Brett, you've watched enough TV; they all say that."

"We'll be in touch," Brett said, signaling an end to the conversation.

CHAPTER THIRTY-FIVE

New York City, N.Y.
September 9, 2001

9:30 a.m.

Cam figured the detectives would keep Brett and Manny busy for at least twenty minutes; he hustled to the elevator and pushed seven. No one was in the hallway when he exited the elevator, so he went straight for the room and swiped the key card, but nothing happened. "Shit," he muttered as he flipped it over and inserted it again. This time he heard a click and a green light appeared on the lock. He slipped into the room and closed the door behind him.

Cam didn't really know what he was looking for, but he wasn't about to pass up an opportunity to snoop. He already had the number of the apartment house in Greenwich Village; he just hadn't shared it with anyone. A little more information couldn't hurt.

The desk had a bunch of notes scribbled on several pages of a pad. He recognized Mulberry Street; he had given it to Brett last night. The page underneath had directions to the 51st subway station, and under that in large letters, *Maria??*

Cam had never been in a fancy hotel room before and he looked around just soaking in the luxury. He strolled into the bathroom and picked up a towel which he rubbed against his cheek. He couldn't believe how soft it was compared to those he used in his mother's two room apartment where he lived when he was broke, a situation he was in at the present time.

He came back into the main room, sunk into the cozy armchair facing the TV, and fingered the remote for the thirty-two inch Mitsubishi. He glanced at his watch; he'd been here for ten minutes. Time to get out, he thought, but he couldn't resist lying down on one of the plush king size beds before he left.

His body sank smoothly into the mattress as it molded to his body shape and he leaned back with his eyes closed and his hands clasped behind his head. He decided again it was time to leave and got up off the bed, but had an urge to try out the other one. He eased on to it expecting to sink down into its softness, but was surprised that it was hard and felt as if it had a bump in the middle. He got off and ran his hand under the sheet, immediately running into what felt like a towel that had become slightly rolled up. He looked again at his watch and then quickly pulled the sheet down from the head of the bed to its middle.

To his surprise he saw a bath mat, not a towel, which he quickly yanked off the mattress exposing a two foot cross of packing tape. He looked again at his watch; twenty minutes had passed since he had used the key card. He frantically tore the tape off the mattress and found himself looking down at bundles of hundred dollar bills.

Cam had to work fast. He pulled the case off a pillow and began stuffing the wads of bills into it. When the mattress was empty, he looked around the room and caught sight of three New York City phone books. He grabbed them and placed them into the cavity along with a couple wash cloths he borrowed from the bathroom. He closed the incisions by pressing the already used tape back in place before covering them with the bath mat and pulling the sheet back over the treasure hole. Sweat was pouring down Cam's face as he made a bee line to the door with the stuffed pillow case in hand, and let it click shut behind him.

The elevator was located dead center in the hallway and Cam raced toward it. When he was within ten feet, a white light came on above the shiny double doors and a shrill ring met his ears. He looked beyond the elevator and spotted a green sign which read EXIT; he kept on running toward it. As Brett and Manny stepped from the elevator, neither saw Cam simultaneously slip into the stairwell.

Cam knew the detectives were waiting for him in the lobby as he scrambled down to the 6th floor. He peeked through the stairwell door into the hallway and spied a maid at the far end. Directly across from his surveillance position, he spotted a door labeled HOUSEKEEPING. He opened it and went in, finding himself not in a room as he had expected, but rather in a large closet.

There were several shelves containing stacks of clean towels and linens. Cam burrowed an opening into the stack on the bottom shelf and shoved his stuffed pillowcase behind a large pile of sheets. He re-arranged the starched cottons so his pillowcase was completely disguised. He opened the door and peeked again down the hall. The maid was still working the other end and Cam strolled down to her. "Morning," he said.

"Good morning, sir," the maid replied, in a heavy Spanish accent.

"How's business?" he asked.

The woman smiled, "I sorry, Yo no comprendo."

"Hablas español?" Cam asked.

"Si."

Cam went into his native tongue and asked if she was going to use all the clean sheets in the closet. "No," she explained in Spanish, "Those are for tomorrow."

Cam reached into his pocket and pulled out a dollar bill, the largest he had, and handed it to the her. "Buenos dias," he said, and walked off toward the elevator.

Pat and Al were waiting for him as he exited into the lobby. "Find anything?" Pat asked.

"Nada," Cam replied.

"English please," Al said, "There must have been something."

"Just a note with Mulberry St. written on it."

"What do they want you to do for them today?" Pat asked.

"Just hang around Mulberry where I lost the babe and see if I spot her."

"Then what?"

"Follow her to an address and apartment number."

"If you get it, what's the first thing you do?"

"Call you man, I'm not stupid."

"It's nine-thirty. You call us at two with or without information, get it?" Al said.

"Got it," Cam replied, and waved goodbye as he pulled a pack of Newports from his shirt pocket.

CHAPTER THIRTY-SIX

New York City, N.Y.
September 9, 2001

11:00 a.m.

Brett knew it wouldn't take long before he received the call. "What are you trying to pull, Raven?" the now familiar distorted voice said. "Half the money is missing from the case."

"You noticed," Brett replied. "Did you really think I'd give you all the money without knowing how I'm getting Annie back?"

"We're not happy."

"Oh, I'm really sorry to hear that, since my main reason for being in New York is to keep you happy. I think it's time you figure out how to insure Annie's return and then you'll get the other half."

There were muffled sounds that were finally broken by the usual voice. "We'll arrange an exchange; how will we know those cops aren't with you?"

"Not my problem. You'll have to figure it out."

"You're awful cocky for a guy with a missing wife. Listen, my friend, and listen good. One person is dead and your wife can easily be added to that list."

Brett backed down. "Okay, I'm not bringing the police, but they're nosing around. The sooner this deal is over, the less the chance of them getting in the way."

"We'll call you back by tomorrow afternoon. Play this right and Annie will be back with you very soon. Play it wrong and we're out of here with only half the money, but also no witnesses."

"I'll wait for your call."

Brett flipped the lid closed on his cell and turned to Manny. "You heard most of it, what do you think?"

"Let's pack up the other million so we'll be ready," Manny replied, as he pulled his own overnight case off the top of the dresser. "We'll use this, it's the right size."

Brett yanked the sheets down and threw the bath mat on the ground. "Oh, oh, this doesn't look right," he said, noticing the tape was barely stuck to the mattress.

Manny rushed over to the bed, ripped the tape off the mattress cut, and out popped a telephone book. His eyes took on a glazed look. "That little shit Cam," he said, as he examined the hole stuffed with wash cloths and phone directories.

All the blood drained from Brett's face. "Manny, we need that money for the exchange tomorrow."

Manny was silent, running the last hour through his brain. "Pretty convenient: the cops keep us busy, they kick Cam out of the coffee shop, he has a key to our room, and the money is gone."

"You think O'Hara and Czychowitz were in on it?"

"They must have given Cam the key, but I doubt they were after money. I think the little prick stumbled on it, scooped it up, and ran."

"What do we do?" Brett asked, as beads of perspiration were forming on his upper lip.

"We don't have much of a choice. Now we need those detectives more than they need us."

"What do you mean?"

"We need them to find Cam before he skips New York with our money, and those detectives are the only ones who know where to look. You still have their cards?"

Brett fumbled through the notes and papers on the desk. "Here they are," he said, as he popped the lid of his cell open and began punching in numbers.

"Czychowitz here, what can I do for ya?"

"It's Brett Raven."

Brett could almost feel the smirk in his voice.

"Dr. Raven, what could possibly be the reason to honor us with this call?"

Brett knew this wouldn't be easy, but he sucked it up. "I need your help," he replied.

"He needs our help, Pat," Brett heard him say to his partner. "I thought you were too smart to ask the police for help, since we don't know shit, right?" he said.

Brett ignored the insult, "Something's come up and I think we can help each other."

"Yeah, how?"

"How long will it take you to get to the St. Regis?"

"Five minutes."

"Meet us in the bar next to the lobby."

"We're making a U turn right now."

Brett and Manny took a booth in the rear of the lounge and Manny ordered a Dos Equis. "Make it two," Brett said, to the waitress.

The detectives arrived at the same time as the beers, their shoulder holsters popping into view as they slid onto the leather seats facing Brett and Manny. "You guys allowed to have a beer on duty?" Brett asked.

"Only if you're buying," Czychowitz replied.

Brett caught the waitress's eye and held up two fingers. A couple more beers were immediately set on the table. "Thanks," O'Hara said, ignoring the glass that came with the beer, as he took a pull from the bottle.

"Yeah, thanks," Czychowitz managed, through a belch. "This why you called us? To become drinking buddies?"

"We need to find Cam," Manny said.

"Really, I didn't know he was lost," O'Hara responded.

"Someone gave him a key to our room. Any idea who?" Brett asked.

Czychowitz downed half the bottle in one gulp. "Yeah, we did."

"Why?" Manny asked.

"Obvious, isn't it? You want to find the kidnappers and we want to find the killers. We all know we're looking for the same people, and since you won't share your info with us, we have to get it any way we can."

"And what did Cam tell you he found?" Manny asked, knowing it wasn't much.

"Said the suspects were probably holed up in Greenwich Village, somewhere near Mulberry," O'Hara replied. "You have more?"

"Maybe," Brett said, while putting up four fingers in the waitress's direction.

"Damn it," Czychowitz said. "You called us over here and the only thing you've given us is a couple beers. What the hell do you want?"

"Cam stole the final ransom payment from us, a million dollars." Brett replied.

"So that's it," Czychowitz smirked. "You need us to find the Chameleon for you."

"Somethin' like that," Manny chimed in.

"You mean, exactly like that," O'Hara said. "What do we get if we find him?"

Brett sat looking down and tapping his index finger on the table top. Finally, he said, "We've already given the kidnappers a million down payment and the other mil is probably due tomorrow. If you get us Cam and we get the money back, we'll give them to you after the exchange for my wife is complete."

"Give us a minute, will you, gentlemen," O'Hara said.

Brett and Manny slid out of the booth and headed for the lobby. "We'll go to the head, be back in five minutes," Brett said, looking back over his shoulder

Brett washed his hands and plucked a white cloth hand towel off a pile neatly arranged on the marble counter top. "Think they can find him?"

"I hope so, anyway, what choice do we have?" Manny replied, imitating a basketball player as he jumped and tossed his towel through the opening in the vanity.

"None, let's get back."

The detectives had serious looks on their faces. "Tell us the deal again; we're not exactly sure how we get our suspects," Pat said.

Brett had most of his beer left and took a couple swallows. "The first thing we need is the money, without that there's no exchange. After I get instructions from the kidnappers, I'll let you know the time and place. You guys know New York; you should be able to set up a trap so they don't get away. Once I have my wife back, you can step in and they're all yours."

"Why do you even need the money if we're goin' to grab 'em?" Al asked.

"There's always a chance they're expecting this; they know you guys have been on us since we stepped off my plane. I want insurance to get my wife back. If you guys screw up, I want them to see the money in the overnight case and have no reason to hang on to her."

"We won't screw up," Al said, defiantly.

Manny joined in, "Yeah, like you cops never make mistakes."

"Fuck you, you hood. Frankly I don't trust you to keep from screwing it up."

Manny stood up, leaned across the table and slammed the palm of his hand into Al's chest. "Fuck you, dick, I don't trust you either."

Czychowitz grabbed Manny forearm and yanked

him onto the table top and cocked his closed fist making ready to strike. "Whoa, whoa," Pat said, as he pulled Al back onto the seat. "What the hell are you doing?"

"I'm not here to take shit from this small time gangster from California," Al replied, as he smoothed his shirt where Manny had ruffled it.

"Come on outside," Pat said, getting up and signaling Al to follow.

Czychowitz did as he was told, but as he was following Pat toward the lobby he turned around and mouthed his lips at Manny, "I'm goin' to get you asshole." Manny put up the middle finger of his right hand and blew him a kiss.

Brett and Manny sat silently nursing their beers, waiting for the return of the detectives. It didn't take long; they slid back into the booth with Pat taking the seat nearest to Manny and nudging Al towards the back of booth. "Sorry," Al said, through lips that appeared semi-paralyzed.

"Yeah, whatever," Brett said, as he looked at his watch. "You sent Cam to our room about nine-thirty; we got back there at five after ten. It's just about noon right now. That's less than two hours. He hasn't had time to sell the money."

"Wait a minute," O'Hara said. "We talked to Cam right after he left your room and he wasn't carrying anything. He must have stashed it in the hotel somewhere."

"You think?" Brett asked.

"Had to," Czychowitz said, finally getting rid of the pout from his face. "Hey, what did you mean by 'sell the money,' why would he sell money?"

Brett looked at Manny and Manny nodded back. "Because the money is counterfeit, at least most of it," Brett said.

Al smiled for the first time since sitting down, "Cam stole a million dollars in funny money?" He began to laugh and continued until he worked himself into hiccups.

"Exactly," Brett replied, not appreciating Al's excitement.

"Does he know that?" Pat asked.

"He'll find out soon enough if he tries to pass it."

"I've got an idea," Pat said. "What if we flush Cam back into the open? He'll have to come back here to retrieve the cash, and he'll lead you guys to where it's hidden."

"Wh...wh...when are the kidnappers calling you back?" Al asked, while trying to hold his breath long enough to stifle the involuntary spasms in his throat.

"This afternoon, the exchange is tomorrow."

Pat got up from the table and motioned Al to follow. "Keep your eyes open," he said to Brett and

Manny. "If things go right, the Chameleon will be slithering back here in a couple hours."

CHAPTER THIRTY-SEVEN

New York City, N.Y.
September 9, 2001

12:10 p.m.

After leaving the hotel, Pat jumped on FDR Drive and headed north. "Give a call to the 25th precinct; they cover Spanish Harlem. Maybe they have an address," Pat said.

Al had it stored in his phone. "NYPD twenty-fifth, Sergeant Rangle," the voice answered.

"Sarg, this is Detective Czychowitz, homicide Midtown South."

"That the famous Albert Czychowitz?"

"Yeah, who's this again?"

"Al, it's me Ray, Ray Rangle. I saved your ass a couple years ago when you lost that evidence from our locker."

"Ray, I'm sorry I didn't pick up the name. Don't remind me, I swear that's the only time that's happened."

"Yeah, yeah, that's what they all say. How ya been?"

"Good, I'm good, but I have to ask another favor."

"I never got the bottle for the last one."

"You didn't? Shit! Tell you what, get me a name and address and I'll send you a case."

"You wouldn't be bullshitting a bull shitter now, would you?"

"Promise, the guy's name is Angel Clemente. I think he lives with his mother up near you in Spanish Harlem. Could you run it real quick?"

"Don't have to."

"What d'ya mean?"

"I know Cam really well; he's a regular guest of ours. His mother's name is Theresa Acosta. 'Don't know what happened to the original Mr. Clemente."

"Got an address?"

"Did you say a full case?"

Al rolled his eyes at Pat, "Yeah, yeah, a full case."

"22337 112th, not sure of the apartment number."

"Thanks, Ray, I owe you."

"Don't owe me, pay me."

"Will do, see ya."

Al switched his phone off speaker. "Get that?"

"Got it," Pat replied. "We're just about in East Harlem."

The streets of Spanish Harlem were lined with large old cars squeezed bumper to bumper into small parking spaces. O'Hara wasn't concerned and pulled up next to a hydrant and tossed an NYPD placard under the windshield. Two, two, three, three, seven, was a tenement apartment house built in the 1950's. It looked as though it had been there since the 1850's. The bricks, originally light brown, had turned almost black from fifty years of exposure to smog, soot and exhaust. Spray painted all over the front of the building was graffiti praising the Harlem Lords, a gang that operated in this Puerto Rican micro-culture.

Theresa Acosta lived three flights up by way of a narrow staircase, that had Al breathing heavily as they approached her door. A teenage girl with olive skin and big brown eyes responded to the detective's knock. "'Help you?" She asked.

Both detectives flipped open wallets exposing gold shields. "NYPD, is Angel Clemente here?" Pat asked.

The young girl looked worried. "He's not here; I'm his sister, is he in trouble?"

"No, Miss, we just need to talk to him. Any idea where we can find him?"

"He left early this morning, ain't seen him since."

A stooped over woman who looked about seventy, but was probably only fifty, approached the door. "What 'chu want with Angel?" She asked in broken English.

"Just need to ask him some questions ma'am," Al said.

"'Bout what?"

"Do you know where we can find him?" Al asked.

"Why you cops always after my boy. He ain't never done nothing."

"We're not after him ma'am. We just have to talk to him, honest," Pat said, as he tried to peek around the two females.

"He ain't here, so don't you bother lookin'." She said, fanning her hand in Pat's face.

"Mind if we come in and take a look?"

"I'll tell him you was lookin' for him when I see him," the older woman said.

Pat took a card from his wallet and handed it to her. "Tell him to call me right away. Tell him I need to know about a sack of missing money. He knows me, we're great friends."

"I'll bet you is," the old woman said, as she snatched the card, while shoving the girl back into the apartment and slamming the door.

"What'd ya think?" Al asked.

"I think Cam will have the message before we

get back to the car."

Al got into the passenger seat. "Better stop at that liquor store on 96th. I'll send Ray a case of Old Crow."

Pat laughed, "Old Crow? We would only drink that crap when a couple dollars was all we could scrape together."

"Ain't like he took a bullet for me." Al said.

Chapter Thirty-Eight

New York City, N.Y.
September 9, 2001

12:30 p.m.

"What do we do if we don't get the money back?" Brett asked Manny.

"Don't even think about it; we'll get it back."

"What makes you so sure?"

"O'Hara and 'Angry Al' know they're getting close, but they need us as partners. They have to flush Cam into the open to do that. They'll get it done, believe me!"

"Really think Cam will go for it?"

"He's so predictable. I feel like a jerk letting him get his hands on the money in the first place. I should have seen that coming. As soon as he knows the cops are after him, he'll want to run, but not before he comes back for the dough. That's more money than he'll ever see in his lifetime."

Brett felt a little better. "How do you want to

set up the lookout?"

"I checked with the desk, there are only two entrances. The main one through the front doors into the lobby and a rear one on the other side of the bar," Manny replied. "I'll take the back, you take the lobby. We can't let him spot us, so lay low, but if you catch sight of him, call me on my cell. I'll do the same."

Brett took up a position with an unobstructed view of the front doors, while still allowing him to be partially hidden by a floor to ceiling plant, which was situated next to the couch he was parked on. He picked up the sports section from the Times that had been left on an end table and tucked his head behind it.

Manny spotted a baseball cap that had been left on the coat rack near the entrance to the bar. He plucked it off the peg and put it on, pulling the bill down close to his eyebrows. He ordered a Stella Artois, took a seat at a small table in the bar, that had a partial view of the back door, and began his vigil.

Manny was working on a second beer and looked at his watch. He'd been in the bar for an hour and twenty minutes and the rear door to the hotel had opened dozens of times, but no Cam.

Suddenly the door opened, but no one came in. Manny pulled the cap lower over his face. The door opened again and someone entered the hotel but stopped in a visual dead spot between the door and the bar. A head quickly peeked out and just as quickly pulled back. The door opened again and the person was gone. Manny hit his speed dial. "Brett, keep an eye out, I think he's headed your way."

"Did you see him?' Brett asked.

"I didn't see him, but he may have seen me. Keep your eyes peeled."

There was frequent traffic coming in and out the front doors, but most of the people were well-dressed and affluent in appearance. Cam will stand out like a sore thumb, Brett thought.

Brett had his eyes riveted on the double glass doors when he spotted something strange. It was an unusually hot September day in New York. Most people were dressed in lightweight clothing, but one guy who was coming into the hotel was dressed in an old wool suit, no tie, tennis shoes, and a fedora pulled down low on his forehead. That has to be him, Brett thought.

To his surprise, the strangely dressed guy headed straight in his direction and Brett knew it was too late to hide, so he buried his head deeper into the newspaper. "Excuse me, sir," a voice on the other side of the paper said.

Brett slowly lowered the sports page.

Expecting to encounter Cam he said, "Okay you little jerk, where is it?"

The guy had taken off his hat; he was almost bald and had a red birthmark on his scalp and looked nothing like the Chameleon. "Sir, I'm a little down on my luck," he said. "Any chance you could spare a buck or two?"

The bald man was obstructing Brett's view of the doors and he wanted him out of his way quickly, so he stood up and reached into his pocket for a dollar. Just as the guy took the bill from Brett's hand, Brett spotted Cam scooting through the lobby and into an elevator. "Nice try," Brett said, as he snatched his dollar back. "I'd stay away from that asshole if I were you."

Brett pulled his cell from his pocket and hit the speed dial for Manny as he raced toward the elevator. "He just got in an elevator, it stopped at four. Wait a minute, again at six."

"Take it to six, I'll take the stairs to four," Manny said. "Don't hang up."

Brett stepped out of the elevator and into the sixth floor hallway, but no sight of Cam. "You still there?" he said, into the open cell phone.

"Yeah," Manny replied, sucking hard for a breath. "I'm on four, and I just opened the door from the stairwell."

"See anything?" Brett asked.

"Hall's empty. Stay where you are, I'll work my way up to you."

"Okay, I'll stay put."

Two minutes later the sixth floor stairway door opened and Manny entered the hall. "No sign of him," he said.

They stood in silence, each man combing his brain for an answer. Suddenly Brett pursed his lips and put his finger to his mouth. "Hear that?" he whispered.

Manny cupped his hand to his ear and then pointed to the door labeled Housekeeping. They both edged toward it just as it popped open.

"Hi Cam, what's with the pillow case? Brett asked. "Helping out the maid?"

Cam's eyes opened wide as saucers and the color drained from his face like air from a leaking balloon. "Oh, hi guys, hi......I can explain," he said, in a weak voice.

"I'll bet you can," Manny replied, while slowly transforming his right hand into a fist.

"Wait a minute, Manny, I want to hear this," Brett said, as he relieved Cam of the stuffed pillowcase.

"Okay, Señor Clemente, let's hear it," Manny said.

Tears began to roll down Cam's face. He tried to wipe them with the back of his hand, but he couldn't keep up with the stream. "I, I," was all that came out of his mouth.

"I told you who the money belongs to, didn't I?" Manny said.

"The, the mob," Cam replied, with his voice cracking.

"And what happens when you steal from the mob?" Manny asked.

Cam sunk to the floor on knees. "Please, guys, I'm sorry, don't turn me in, please," he said, with his hands clamped together in a praying position.

Manny looked at Brett. "Your call."

"You blew it Cam, you got greedy. Now get out and don't let us see you around here again," Brett said.

Cam got up off his knees. "Thank you, guys, thanks." He quickly went for the elevator, pushed the down button and looked back. "You don't think I could get part of the grand you promised?"

Manny's face took on an angry look as he moved toward Cam. "Just kiddin'," Cam said, as he scooted through the elevator doors that had just opened.

CHAPTER THIRTY-NINE

New York City, N.Y.
September 10, 2001

10:45 a.m.

Maria spotted him the minute she walked out the front door of the apartment building on Mulberry. He was smoking a cigarette while propped up against a light post and was doing a poor job of pretending to be reading a newspaper. The print was upside down. "I know you, don't I?" Maria said, walking directly up to him.

"Who me?" the man asked, faking an incredulous look of bewilderment.

Maria looked up and down the street. "You see anyone else on this block?"

"I don't know you, honest. I don't even know who you are. Who are you?"

"I'm either your best friend or your worst enemy. Which is it going to be?"

Cam took one last puff from his Newport and

using his thumb and forefinger flicked it out into the street. "Hey, you must have me mixed up with someone else."

"You were in Kinko's the day I was there, and you followed me off the subway the other night. I don't think I have you mixed up with anyone."

Cam could feel the droplets of perspiration as they broke through the cloth of his already stained shirt. "Should we, uh, talk?"

"We are talking. Who are you, who do you work for, and what do you want?" Maria asked.

As scared as he was, Cam couldn't help staring down at the perfect cleavage formed by Maria's bulging breasts restrained by the tight open necked, sleeveless blouse she was wearing. "Get your eyes off me," she commanded. "This stuff's way out of your league."

"Hey, just looking; no big deal."

"Answer my questions, who are you and who do you work for?"

"Name's Cam, I used to work for Raven and his buddy, but we parted ways," He blurted out.

Maria looked him up and down trying to figure out why Brett would hire this loser. "Who are you working for now?" she asked.

"Myself," Cam answered, while keeping his eyes averted and trying desperately to remove his last smoke from the pack.

"How much?" Maria asked.

"What d'ya mean, how much?"

"You don't work for free do you? You're here because you smell money. How much do you smell?"

"You mean not to tell Raven where you're holed up?"

"You're catching on, how much?"

Cam managed to get the cigarette lit and inhaled a deep cloud of smoke. "I figure you already picked up a million. How 'bout you cut me a hundred thou," he said, as he exhaled all but the tar and the nicotine.

Maria broke out laughing. "We'd kill you before we gave you a hundred thousand dollars."

Cam hadn't thought of that possibility and was immediately remorseful for his demand. "Uh, how 'bout twenty K."

"You ever see a dead guy?' Maria asked.

"Once, why?"

"It's not a pretty sight. We left one behind in a hotel room."

"Why you tellin' me this?"

"Because I want you to know we're killers. Now, once more, how much?"

The term 'never let 'em see you sweat' didn't apply to Cam. There were huge circles of perspiration forming on his light blue shirt, stretching from the armpits to the shoulders. "I'm easy, how 'bout a thousand?" he managed to say, even though his mouth felt as if it was filled with wads of cotton.

"I'll give you two, but you'll have to earn it."

"How?" he asked.

"When the time is right, I want you to give Raven our address and apartment number."

"Really, why?"

"Don't ask questions. Do you want the job or not?"

"Sure, sure I do. That all I have to do?"

"That's all," Maria replied, as she opened her purse and took out ten one hundred dollar bills. She handed them to Cam. "If you do good you get the other thousand, if you do bad we're going to kill you."

Cam gently snatched the money from Maria's grasp. "You'll tell me when?" he asked, while counting the bills.

Maria reached into her purse and removed a pack of post-its and a pencil. "Write your cell number down and wait to hear from me early tomorrow."

"Sure, sure, how do I get the rest of the money?"

"You'll get it when we know we don't have to kill you."

Cam jotted a set of numbers on the sticky and handed it back to Maria. "That's cool, that's cool, early tomorrow, right?"

"Pick up on the first ring," Maria said, and walked away.

CHAPTER FORTY

New York City, N.Y.
Sept. 10, 2001

1:35 p.m.

The call arrived. "Are you ready to make the exchange?" The eerie voice asked.

"Of course I'm ready," Brett replied. "What are the instructions?"

"You'll receive a call early tomorrow morning giving you an address and apartment number. Take the money to that address."

"Wait a minute! We agreed I would be assured of getting my wife back when I deliver the money."

"She'll be in the apartment."

"I don't get it, who do I give the money to?"

"We'll be there with her. You come in, deliver the money and we deliver the key to her locked up bedroom. We won't be hanging around for the reunion."

Brett was confused, something wasn't right.

"Not good enough, I want to talk to her. Now!"

"Don't get excited. If we let you talk to her, will you be satisfied we'll deliver her safely?" Brett was silent. "Look Raven, we don't want your wife, we only want the money."

Brett looked toward Manny, who was listening to the speaker phone. He nodded. "Okay, let me talk to her."

"Hold on," the voice said. There was muted mumbling in the background as Brett waited. Finally, a new distorted voice came through the earpiece. "Brett?"

"Annie, is that you?"

"Yes, yes, it's me."

"Annie, I can't recognize your voice through that machine. I have to know it's really you." He thought for a moment. "Do you remember the name of the hotel we stayed in when we visited Florence?"

She paused a few seconds and then blurted, "The Lung... Lungarno."

"Oh, Honey, I've missed you. Are you okay?"

"I'm a little unkempt, but I'm fine; nothing the hairdresser and manicurist can't fix. I've missed you too."

"They say if I drop the money, they'll let you go. Should I trust them?"

"The money is all they want, but can we afford it?"

"Don't worry about the money, I have it under control."

A new voice took Annie's place. "That's it, do we have a deal?"

"Let me say goodbye," Brett said.

There was another pause and then Annie came back on. "They say we'll be together again by noon tomorrow, I can't wait."

Brett was holding back tears. "I love you, hon. I'll see you tomorrow."

The voice was back. "Do we have a deal or not?"

"I'll wait for the call tomorrow morning. The money will be in an overnight case."

"Perfect, and the same as the last payment, negotiable hundred dollar bills."

"It's ready and waiting for delivery."

"Good, remember if we see cops you'll never see Annie alive again. We don't want to, but we've killed once, we can do it again." The phone went silent.

Brett dialed O'Hara's number. He answered with his usual greeting, "O'Hara."

"It's Brett Raven."

"We've been waiting for your call. Did we flush the little weasel out?"

Brett laughed at the detectives two word description, it was perfect. "Yeah, it worked, we got the money back."

"Did your buddy beat the shit out of him?"

"Why? Cam's just a pathetic soul. Nothing to be gained there."

"Easy to say once you got the money back. I'd hate to see what his face would like if he hadn't given up the dough.

"Well, he did," Brett replied.

"Okay, Raven, it's your turn to deliver. You promised us the killers."

"I know, I know. I just have to be convinced you guys won't get impatient and close in too early. I think they're capable of harming my wife if they smell cops."

"You think we're rookies? We've been here before, we know how to close. Did they call with instructions?"

"Yes, but the address for the money drop isn't coming 'til early tomorrow morning. They said Annie will be in that apartment."

"That's a little strange, why would your wife be at the drop site? They'd have to expose themselves to pick up the money."

"I wondered that myself. You think maybe the apartment is just a test and it will send me somewhere else?"

"That's what I'm thinking. They give you a hint where the location is?"

"No, but I'm guessing in Greenwich Village

somewhere.   The little weasel was good for something.”

Brett could hear O’Hara talking to Czychowitz, so he waited, knowing they were discussing strategy. After a couple minutes O’Hara was back on the line. “Okay, we’re all goin’ to be ready by 4 a.m.   No telling what ‘early tomorrow’ really means. After you get the address, call us. We’ll park ourselves on the street, not looking like cops. Call me again before you get there and keep the phone on and in your shirt pocket. If anyone is really there, we want to hear any conversation that takes place. If they’re stupid enough to meet you face to face and exchange your wife for the money, we’ll move in.”

“Not sooner, promise?”

“Promise,” O’Hara said, knowing he may not be able to keep it.

“Okay, we’ll talk early tomorrow.” Brett ended the call and turned to Manny. “How do you feel about it?”

“I’m a little concerned why the money would be dropped where Annie is being held, but we have no choice. We go with it. Just in case of a screw up, though, while the cops are watching you, I’ll be watching them.”

“Did you bring a gun?” Brett asked with trepidation.

Manny broke out in laughter. "Come on, Brett, Enrique sent me as a bodyguard. Only a fool goes into battle without a weapon," he said.

"Don't go shooting any cops with it."

"I wouldn't mind giving Czychowitz a good pop, but don't worry, I'm too smart for that."

Brett went to the mini-bar and took out two miniatures of Maker's Mark. He unscrewed the caps of both bottles and handed one to Manny. "To success," he said with a frown as he tapped his bottle to Manny's.

Manny tapped back. "Brett, don't worry, we're going to be successful," he said, as he took a long pull from the little bottle.

Brett drained half of his whiskey. "You're a good friend, Manny. In case I don't get a chance to say it tomorrow, thanks. Thanks for everything."

"You're welcome, but you're sounding like this is a suicide mission. Cheer up."

"Sure Manny, but I just have a feeling tomorrow may be a bad day."

"Don't worry," Manny said with confidence. "Tomorrow will be just another day."

Chapter Forty-One

New York City, N.Y.
September 10, 2001

2:00 p.m.

"Why'd you promise him that," Al asked.

Pat shot him a guilty look. "What should I have said? 'It's our call and we'll move in whenever the hell we want to.' He'd cut us right out of the deal."

"So, it is our call?"

"Absolutely, we'll do what we have to do to get those killers."

Czychowitz smiled knowing that asshole Manny wouldn't get the best of him. "I still don't get the setup, do you?"

"You mean why they would have the wife where they pick up the money?"

"Yeah, exactly. Why would they show their faces, release the wife, and then think Raven would just give them a million dollars and let them walk away with it. Somethin' is fishy."

O'Hara reached in his pocket and ferreted out a cigarette butt. "You're right, it's a formula for getting caught. Especially when they suspect we'll be on Raven's tail."

Czychowitz laughed. "You're not going to smoke that?"

Pat turned it over in his hand. "Pretty pathetic, isn't it? I made a deal with my wife. I promised I'd only have one a day and she promised not to bug me about it. This is left over from this morning."

"Big deal, she won't know, light a fresh one."

Pat gave Al a forlorn look and lit the butt with a Zippo he pulled from his pocket. "I promised," he said. "How many of those can I break in twenty-four hours?"

Al didn't see it as a problem but let it go. "So how do you think it will go down tomorrow morning?"

O'Hara took a deep drag which burned the paper all the way down to his fingertips. He felt the heat and dropped the cinder to the ground and stepped on it. "No way they'll risk getting caught. I doubt the wife or the kidnappers will be in that apartment," he said, as he exhaled a gray cloud of smoke with a look of pleasure.

"So it's just a diversion to send Raven somewhere else."

"Sure, they'll be watching to make sure no cops are around and then they'll give him new directions. He'll have no choice. He wants his wife back. He'll comply."

"So what d' we do?"

"We stick to plan. We'll stake out in disguise and just let it play out."

"Yeah, but once Raven gets new directions he'll be on the move. How do we get back to the car in time?"

"Hey, I'll be monitoring his cellphone. As soon as we're sure nothing's going down in the apartment, we head for the car. The odds we get a killer from that apartment are probably a million to one."

"Why even bother staking the place? Maybe we should just concentrate on following Raven after he leaves."

"I didn't say the odds were zero, I said a million to one. Let's not throw away our lottery ticket, who knows, maybe it's the winner."

"Doubt it," Czychowitz said.

CHAPTER FORTY-TWO

New York City, N.Y.
Aug. 30, 2001

11 days ago .....

"What did ya order for dinner?" Biff asked.

"Steak for us, chicken for her," J.T. said, pointing to the closed door leading to the extra bedroom.

"Anything to drink?"

"Few beers for us. Diet for her."

"How long ya think before we see the money?" Biff asked.

"A week, maybe ten days max. He'll need some time to liquidate and get from California to New York."

Biff motioned toward the bedroom. "We goin' to keep her holed up the entire time?"

"What choice do we have?"

Biff shrugged. "She goin' nuts?" he asked

"Watches a lot of television I picked up a bunch

of paperbacks from the hotel shop for her to read."

"What's the chances they'll call the cops after this is over?"

"They're scared shitless about those unborn babies. We'll be fine.

J.T. heard a soft knock on the door. "Get that, will you, our dinner's here. I have to hit the head."

Biff opened the door and a young guy in a navy blue, very over used uniform, pushed a metal cart into the room. "Want it set up on the table?" he asked.

"Yeah, set it for three," Biff replied, knowing full well Annie would be eating in her room. "Grab me one of those beers first."

The bellhop passed a Coors Lite to Biff and began setting the table just as J.T. came out of the bathroom. He examined the check and extracted $140 in bills from his wallet to cover the $127 total, along with an extra $13 for the server. He handed the cash to him and said, "Thanks, man, nice job."

"Thank you sir," the bellhop replied, as he backed the cart out the door.

J.T. took a plastic tray that was left with the food delivery and loaded it with a salad, the chicken plate and a diet Coke. "Biff, unlock that door for me, will you."

Biff fiddled with the makeshift lock J.T. had devised until it finally popped open, and then he pushed the door inward. As soon as the door was halfway open, a wooden handle hair brush was delivered airborne and hit Biff in the forehead, opening up a cut just above his right eyebrow. "You bastards, let me out of here," Annie yelled, watching Biff use his index finger to wipe the trickle of blood from his eyelid.

"You want dinner or not?" J.T. asked, nudging Biff out of the doorway.

"What is it? Bread and water," Annie replied.

"I told you, just relax and this will be over in a few days."

"Brett's too smart; he'll never go for this."

"You're wrong about that, he already has."

"I don't believe you," Annie said venomously.

"You know, Annie, I don't really care what you think. I just want some of my money back."

"You still insist it's your money, like you worked for it. You stole it!"

Feeling uncomfortable, J.T. changed the direction of the conversation. "Do you remember when we loved each other?"

"Did we ever, really?"

"Well, I can't speak for you, but I was in love."

"You were never in love with me. The only person you've ever loved is yourself."

"That's insulting."

"If you loved me so much, why did you take up

with Maria and run out on me?"

"At that point our marriage was over, but I thought leaving you a $5 million dollar life insurance policy would ease the pain."

"Damn you, you've always measured everything in terms of dollars, even love. Besides, the policy was bogus, you weren't really dead."

"Nobody knew that until Brett started nosing around."

"He started nosing around because he thought you were getting a bum rap for crashing that airplane. He thought he would salvage the reputation of a long lost friend."

J.T.'s episode of nostalgia was over. "Annie, I don't want to hurt you or your unborn babies, but we're going to get that money even if some violence is necessary. I told you I was desperate, and I am. Don't ever forget that."

Annie grabbed the corner of the tray and flipped it over, spilling the food down the front of J.T.'s trousers. "Screw you and screw that fat slob who's helping you. You're both going to end up in jail or dead."

J.T. slammed the door shut and clicked the lock. "Bitch," he mumbled.

"She's a little feisty," Biff said, pleased that he was not the only recipient of Annie's wrath.

"Believe me, she's the least of your worries."

"What does that mean?" Biff asked.

"Nothing, just stay focused on the end game, that's all."

Biff shrugged, sat down at the table, popped another beer and began digging into his steak. "Gonna eat?"

"Yeah, right after I change these pants."

Biff didn't wait for J.T. to return from the bedroom and continued to work on his T-bone. Suddenly his attention was diverted to the main door where a gentle knocking was coming from the hall. He jumped up, and looked at his watch; six o'clock on the nose. He looked through the peephole and recognizing the distorted image, opened the door for Maria. "You're right on time. Is this it?" he asked, as he let her in.

Maria strutted into the room. She looked as if she was attending a business appointment, dressed in a blue suit, white blouse, blue pumps and white gloves which were grasping a black shoulder bag. "This is it," she replied. "Where is he?"

"In the bedroom, our guest threw her dinner all over him. Where's the Beretta?"

She patted the side of her bag twice. "Right here."

"I...I'm still not real comfortable with this," Biff mumbled.

"Too late, partner, you already agreed to it.

Don't worry; I won't make the big tough marine pull the trigger. At least someone has the balls for it since you obviously don't."

Biff's face flushed pink in reaction to the insult, but he knew it was true and had no retort, so instead he said, "He'll be surprised to see you here. How ya going to handle it?"

"Just take a seat. You'll see."

Biff seated himself back at the table and Maria settled into the chair without a place setting in front of it. They waited in silence. The quiet didn't last long. J.T. came out of the bedroom buckling his belt on a fresh pair of khakis. His attention was diverted toward Annie's door where food was congealing on the floor in front of it. Not even noticing the new occupant to the suite, he glanced up saying, "Hey, Biff, couldn't you clean..." and then he saw her. "Maria, wha...what are you doing here?"

"Hello, hubby, you happy to see me?"

"Well yes, but how...?"

Biff was getting nervous. He'd seen plenty of dead guys during his stint in the marines, and he probably even killed a few, but he'd never been this up close and personal. He pushed his chair a few inches back from the table.

"I ran into Biff a while back, didn't he tell you?" Maria said.

J.T. looked perplexed and turned to Biff. "I don't get it, what the hell?"

"Sit down, my love," Maria said. "Let me bring you up to speed."

J.T. sat down, his upper lip showing a bead of sweat. Biff pushed back a few more inches anticipating a messy scene.

"I have another surprise for you," Maria said, as she slid the clasps down to release the large flap on her leather bag. She eased her white gloved hand into the purse, withdrew the cold black Beretta, and with precision, attached the silencer to the end of its barrel.

"Maria! What in God's name?" J.T. Yelled.

"Two million isn't nearly enough to split three ways, is it Biff?" Maria asked, as she pointed the pistol at J.T.

"No way," Biff replied, now feeling secure with the situation which Maria literally had in hand.

"Maria, I'm still your husband. Don't do this!" J.T. pleaded his voice an octave above normal.

"You've never taken marriage vows too seriously anyway, have you darling?"

"I, I…" J.T. stammered.

"What do you think Biff, should we reduce the number of players from three to two?" Maria asked.

"I'm good with it," Biff replied, leaning back another inch or two in his chair.

"Maria placed her other gloved hand on the Beretta to steady it and as Biff glanced away from the confrontation, she moved the barrel in his direction and pulled the trigger, putting a silenced bullet into his forehead. The chair came out from under him, as he fell to the floor flat on his back, his eyes open in bewilderment.

"We had no choice," Maria said. "He would have hounded us forever."

"I know, we had to!" J.T. replied. We made that decision the day we argued in West Palm, when you left and later came back with this plan." He gave her a kiss. "It was brilliant."

"How long will it take to strip and clean the suite?" Maria asked.

"Maybe an hour. Is the apartment in Greenwich Village ready?"

"All paid for and waiting for us."

"Let's get started, the sooner we get out of here the better."

Chapter Forty-Three

New York City, N.Y.
September 11, 2001

6:30 a.m.

The ring of Cam's cell phone jolted him out of a wonderful dream. His subconscious had him in a romantic embrace with Maria. "Hello," he answered.

"Wake up, you little prick, there's work to do."

"I've been awake for an hour just waiting for your call."

"I doubt that. You have a pen and paper?"

"Sure, sure…got the address?"

"275 Mulberry, apartment 211. The front door entry code is #6565."

"Got it."

"Read it back," Maria ordered.

"Uh…two, seven..what?"

Maria had no\patience, "275, get it right. 275 Mulberry."

"Okay, okay I got it. 275 Mulberry, number 211, code #6565," Cam said.

"This is serious, my friend, your life could depend on getting this right. Make the call to Raven's cellphone at exactly seven-thirty. That's one hour from now. Repeat what I said."

"One hour, seven-thirty."

"What do you know, you got it right.

"Yes, Ma'am, just one more thing."

"What?"

 "Uh, how do I get the rest of my money?"

"If you get this right, pick up an envelope with your name on it at the United counter at Newark Airport. If you don't get it right you better be able to run…fast."

"Is this Raven, that asshole from California?" the caller asked.

"Cam, get off this line, I'm expecting an important call," Brett replied.

A squeaky laugh filled the earpiece. "This is the call, man."

"What are you talking about?"

"For a grand I'll give you the address you've been waiting for."

"How do you know I've been waiting for this call?"

"'Cause the babe told me. Do I get the grand

or not?"

Brett actually gave it a moment's thought before he called Cam's bluff. "No."

"What'cha mean, no?"

"Give me the address, now!"

"Come on, I'm doing you a favor, how 'bout two hundred bucks.

"How 'bout you give me the address and I won't send Manny after you?"

"Okay, but you owe me; 275 Mulberry, apartment 211, door code #6565."

"Thanks Cam, I changed my mind. Stop by later and I'll settle up with you."

Cam thought about the offer for a few seconds. "Uh, no thanks, this one's on me. See ya."

Brett dialed O'Hara's cell. "Here's the address," he said, and then recited it twice. "I should be there about eight fifteen. That going to give you enough time?"

"We'll be up the street. Don't forget, before you go in, dial my number and keep the call active. I'll be listening."

"Will do, remember, if someone's there, don't come in 'til I have Annie."

"I know our bargain, just don't try to be a hero."

"See you in Greenwich Village in an hour."

Manny handed Brett the overnight case with

the $20 thousand genuine currency and $980 thousand counterfeit. "We'll try to get it back after you have Annie."

Brett gave an affirmative nod, knowing that would only be a bonus to getting Annie back.

Manny stepped closer and gave Brett a bear hug. "Cheer up, buddy, we're almost home. Give me a five minute head start to stake out a spot before you get there. Good luck."

"Thanks Manny. Maybe you were right, maybe it'll be a good day after all."

CHAPTER FORTY-FOUR

New York City, N.Y.
September 11, 2001

6:45 a.m.

Maria whipped up scrambled eggs and toast and delivered breakfast to Annie's room. "If your husband is as smart as you say, you'll be with him in a few hours."

"Thank God," Annie replied. "Can you tell me now why I was blindfolded when we left the hotel and why Biff disappeared?

"It's not important. Goodbye, Annie, it's been a pleasure. Enjoy your new babies," she said, as she locked the door behind her.

"I'm headed out to the airport with this first satchel of money. I'll pick up our tickets to San Francisco and tomorrow at this time we'll be in Bora Bora," Maria said to J.T., giving him a kiss on the lips.

"They know the second bag of money has to be

in the airport locker by nine this morning, right?" J.T. asked, merely reviewing the details.

"As soon as I have it, I'll call you. You let Annie go and grab a cab to the Newark terminal. Our plane leaves at noon."

"Can't wait," J.T. said, blowing another kiss toward Maria who was already exiting the front door.

Maria hailed a cab. "Newark Airport," she said, while glancing at her watch, 7:15. "Perfect," she whispered to herself.

Pat was dressed as a summertime tourist, in a Hawaiian shirt, blue Bermuda shorts, black socks, and white sneakers. Al looked like a local in a faded blue running suit, Yankees cap, and white Adidas. They left their car two blocks away and split up, but their destination was the same, 275 Mulberry.

Pat entered the block from the south, taking photos of buildings with a cheap digital camera and appearing to be listening to music through a set of earbuds. Al entered from the north and was working up a sweat as he jogged past Pat. They didn't say a word to each other, both so focused that neither noticed a drunk passed out in an entryway with a bottle of red wine poking out of a paper bag beside him.

The cab pulled to the curb directly in front of the

brick apartment house. Brett looked at the meter, $15.45. He grabbed the overnight case and handed the driver a twenty. "Keep the change," he said, and hurried toward the door. He didn't have to look at his notes. He punched in #6565 and heard the lock click as the door opened a half inch. He went in and as an afterthought, stuffed a Kleenex into the cavity which normally would allow the door to lock behind him. He dialed O'Hara's number and dropped his cell into his shirt pocket.

The apartment house was old and had no elevator. He looked around and rushed to the closed stairwell. As he opened the door, he was met with the stench of perspiration and stale cigarette smoke. It made him gag, and he held his breath as he took two stairs at a time to the second floor.

Brett looked at his watch. It was 8:15 just as he reached apartment 211. Expecting the door to be open, he turned the knob, but nothing happened. He pushed and pulled on the door, hoping if the lock was stuck he could jar it open. "Who is that?" a male voice from inside yelled. Brett stepped back. He wasn't really expecting anyone to be here. "I have the money," he said, to the closed door.

There was no response, but Brett could hear a drawer open and slam shut inside the apartment. He waited, feeling his stomach tighten and his mouth become dry. Suddenly the door opened, and there was J.T. facing him with a pistol in his hand. He had an expression of surprise on his face and looked up and down the hallway checking for any other unexpected visitors. Quickly he motioned Brett to enter and closed the door behind him. "What the hell are you doing here? You were supposed to drop the money in a locker at Newark Airport."

"Locker? Newark Airport? What are you talking about? Cam told me to bring the money here."

"Cam? Who the fuck is Cam?"

Brett was dumbfounded and speechless. Finally, he said, "He's the guy who called and gave me this address for the exchange."

"I don't know any Cam. How would he get this address and how would he know about the ransom?"

"You tell me, he said a 'babe' told him to call me. I've got a pretty good idea who that was. Don't you?"

Now it was J.T.'s turn to be perplexed. "Wha.. what's going on?" He mumbled. The synapses in his gray matter were working overtime until suddenly the fuzzy picture became clear. The noises that came next from his mouth sounded as if they were coming from a wounded animal, guttural and agonizing. "Oh, no, Maria, no, no," he whimpered, through lips that were barely moving. He put his head down and looked as if he was ready to break into tears, and then suddenly his face transformed into a blank, expressionless mask. He pointed to the case that Brett was holding and with no emotion whatsoever left in his voice he asked, "Is that the 2nd million in the case?"

"Yes, it's all here," Brett replied, setting it on a chair.

J.T. opened the case while still holding the barrel of the gun in Brett's direction. He ripped a bill off the top of one of the stacks and reached over for a yellow marker pen that he used to swipe a line across it. He held it up to the light which was filtering in through the window and satisfied of its authenticity, he stuffed it into his pants pocket. "This wasn't the way it was supposed end," he said. "I really didn't want to hurt you or Annie, but now I'm backed into a corner." He reached into his other trouser pocket and took out the silencer which he twisted into place on the barrel of the Beretta.

Brett stepped back. "J.T., this is foolish! Why would you kill us? You have the money!"

"Because you'd never let me get away, I know you. You can never let go. That's the real reason we're here, isn't it? You couldn't mind your own business and stay out of mine. If you hadn't stirred the hornet's nest a year ago, none of this would have happened. Now I'm left with only one choice to get away. I'm really sorry," he said, as he raised the barrel.

"No!" Brett cried out, taking another step back, bracing for a shot to ring out. The door exploded open with the force of a shoulder behind it, and O'Hara burst in with Czychowitz right behind him. Stunned, J.T. turned the Beretta toward the door and fired. O'Hara felt the burn from the bullet as it entered his shoulder and dropped him to the floor. Czychowitz was slow to react and found himself facing a crazed J.T. who now had the pistol leveled straight at him. Another shot rang out!

J.T., with a look of disbelief, dropped the Beretta and used his now free hand to slow the blood that was spurting from his abdomen. His knees buckled from under him as he fell to the carpet. Czychowitz, who hadn't had time to fire his weapon, turned to look behind him. Manny was smiling, holding his Glock up in the firing position with both hands.

Brett could hear pounding coming from one of the bedroom doors. He turned the key and opened it. Annie fell into his arms. "Oh, my God, I heard shots, are you okay?" she screamed.

He hugged her tight. "I'm fine but you don't look very good."

"I've never felt better," she replied, squeezing Brett toward her. "Are our babies okay?"

"I talked to Samantha a couple days ago, they're fine. One more month," he replied, and gave her a kiss.

It only took the paramedics five minutes to reach the apartment after Czychowitz's 9-1-1 call. They were placing dressings on Pat, while J.T., his face ashen gray, was lying unconscious prone on a gurney, when Al finally turned to Manny. "You son of a bitch! You're the last person in this world I want to owe my life to."

Manny smiled, "Life just ain't fair is it?" he said.

Maria's flight was scheduled to leave at 8:42. It was already a little after eight by the time she paid the taxi driver and ran into the terminal. She had gotten her boarding pass yesterday, and now she headed straight for the United departure gate. By the time she reached it, she was the very last to board. Her only luggage was the satchel filled with a million dollars which she reluctantly placed in the overhead compartment and then settled into her seat. The door was latched shut and the flight attendant announced: "Welcome to Flight Ninety-Three from Newark to San Francisco."

CHAPTER FORTY-FIVE

New York Times
September 12, 2001

Yesterday, United Flight 93, from Newark to San Francisco crashed in a field near Shanksville, Pennsylvania. It was believed the hijackers target was the U.S. Capitol or the White House.

MY THANKS

———————

To *Candyce Griswold* for her hours of relentless editing.

To *Carla Resnick* for her skill designing the book's cover and its contents.

To authors, *Lloyd Rogers* and *Douglas Bockus,* for their time reading and praising the manuscript.

To my wife, *Bev* for her counsel and patience every time she heard me ask, "How does this sound?"

To my characters who appeared in the three Brett Raven mystery novels.

My heroes: *Brett, Annie, Manny, Enrique, Ginger.*

My villains: *J.T., Maria, Claude, Biff, the Rivera brothers.*

My supporting cast: *Carmen, Marcella, Drake, Omar, Rob, O'Hara, Czychowitz, Cam, Juan, Janet.*

I have a good idea where some of you came from, others I have no clue. You just seemed to appear.

Mike Paull is a retired dentist from the San Francisco Bay Area and is also a licensed commercial pilot with over thirty-five hundred flying hours. He now resides in Chico, California.

Mike's first book, *Tales from the Sky Kitchen Café*, was published in 2011.

Flight of Betrayal, published in 2012, is the first of the Brett Raven mystery series.

Flight of Deception, published in 2013, is the second in the Brett Raven Trilogy.

Flight of No Return, published in 2014, completes the Brett Raven Mystery Trilogy.

Follow the Brett Raven Mysteries

Facebook
Brett Raven Mysteries

Skyhawk Publishing
skyhawkpublishing.com

E-book format available
Amazon.com
Barnes and Noble.com
Apple Store.com